ALL THE WAY BACK HOME

/ / / /

J.R. RAIN

SELECT BOOKS BY J.R. RAIN

Winter Wind

Silent Echo

The Body Departed

The Grail Quest

Elvis Has *Not* Left the Building

The Lost Ark

Published by
Crop Circle Books
212 Third Crater, Moon

Printed in the United States of America.

ISBN-9781099489044

Chapter One

I might've been slightly drunk when I almost hit the white dog.

Okay, a lot drunk. I probably shouldn't have been driving like this at night, especially on this narrow mountain road while it rained so hard the droplets became slanting silver daggers sweeping before my headlights, obscuring the road ahead of me. Oblivious, I hummed a song of my own invention and wondered if I had any beer at the house or if I should stop at the liquor store just outside of town—when it appeared before me, seemingly hovering above the asphalt like a white ghost. Then again, that could have been the alcohol talking.

I slammed on the brakes and wrenched the wheel to the right. Tires squealed and my Jetta nearly flipped. I waited for the tell-tale thud of hitting the white... something, but the thud never came.

Funny thing, by the end of the slide I felt completely sober.

When the Jetta finally stopped, I opened my eyes and sat there gasping for breath. I had ended up on the muddy shoulder. Stunned and numb, I reached down and turned on my hazard lights. Then pushed open the door and stumbled out into the rain…

***

The white dog…

There it was, aglow in my headlights, looking for all the world like a slumbering polar bear. I approached it cautiously. The closer I got to the pile of white fur—especially as I saw the copious amounts of blood running downhill—the more squeamish I became. In fact, I came close to vomiting… probably the beer talking. I had been, after all, a dentist. I had seen my fair share of blood.

Then again, that had been nearly two years ago…

Anyway, I would have bet good money that the creature was dead, victim of a hit and run. I ran my fingers through my already-drenched hair, and considered doing nothing. That's what guys like me did, right? Guys with nothing to live for did nothing. We went home, drank more, and regretted our decisions all over again.

As I stood there doing nothing, a cold burst of wind lifted the bloodied white fur. Wait… the wind didn't do that. No, its chest rose and fell from breathing.

It was alive.

***

The dog either gasped or panted, although the sound of it drowned under the sizzling rain and the idling engine.

A rivulet of blood wended its way from the dog over the curve of road. A lot of blood. Then again, this was a big dog, too. And male. I could see that pretty obviously. The pink tongue lolled in a pool of bloody rainwater. One side of the face rested in the puddle, the other half exposed to the driving rain. A large brown, unblinking eye watched me.

"Hey buddy," I whispered, stunned.

Amazingly, he lifted his head and water poured down the side of his face. He drew his lips up in a sort of greeting and leveled a stare at me unlike anything I'd ever seen, man or beast. Whoa, unreal. There was a small chance that he'd just looked into my soul. That, or I was passed out drunk and dreaming all this. He lowered his head, obviously too weak or injured to keep it up.

I leaned down and wondered what to do. Comfort the creature in his final moments? Try to help him? Could I even help him? Was I still drunk or not? I mean, I *should* be drunk. I'd certainly had my fill tonight.

And what was with that look?

The creature was beautiful, despite the blood stains. Furry white muzzle. Big floppy ears. Brown eyes with unusually long eyelashes. I couldn't make out the breed... perhaps a shepherd of some sort.

"You having a rough night, pooch?" I asked. As I spoke, the stink of alcohol on my own breath slapped me in the face. My voice sounded distant, hollow, and oddly foreign to my own ears. Like this really wasn't happening. Like I had passed out drunk and was dreaming this whole encounter.

Rainwater dripped from the tip of my nose, falling into the dog's matted fur. Most of the blood seemed to be centered along his abdomen. I reached down, took hold of a forepaw, and gently lifted...

And saw the source of his injury.

Holy sweet Jesus, I'm dreaming.

A long, ugly cut had sliced him open from sternum to belly.

I stared in stunned silence, bewildered, trying to wrap my foggy head around what I was seeing. This dog looked like he'd bolted off the operating table in the middle of surgery. No, not quite an operation. The incision was too jagged a hack job.

The old boy closed his eyes. His pink tongue was flecked with white spittle and streaks of blood. He'd done the only thing he knew how to do: lick his wound clean. Except a dog couldn't lick a gaping hole like this clean. So, what had happened here? I hadn't a clue, but I knew he needed help, or he would bleed out.

I considered calling for help. The police? No, I

would get arrested… again. A friend? Didn't really have any of those left. Family? None. I paused, considering a professor friend of mine, but he lived in Big Bear a half hour away, and I couldn't ask him to drive out on a night like this in the wind and rain, along a winding mountain road thousands of feet high, complete with sheer cliffs.

No, I had no one to turn to for help, no one I could pass this dog off to. Saving this creature fell squarely onto my drunk shoulders. I rubbed a palm down my wet face. I would have been home by now, or close to it. I would have been in bed soon, to sleep deep into tomorrow, only to do the drinking thing all over again.

The dog was going to die, right? I mean, look at that wound. That crazy, incomprehensible wound. The least I could do was get him off the road. Let him die with some dignity, rather than get hit by another drunk screaming along these treacherous roads.

Okay, yeah. I could do that. Yes, I could at least move him.

As if on cue, headlights appeared to my right, coming in the same direction I had been driving. Without thinking, I reached under the dog, vaguely aware that I risked him biting me.

An engine roared, loud. The idiot drove even faster than I had... and I had only barely managed to swerve in time.

When I shifted the dog, trying to get hold of him, he yelped. He was a big boy, well over a hundred pounds, much of that in white fur alone, not to mention wet and dead weight. Lord, help me. Careful of his ghastly wound, I maneuvered him as best as I could into my arms and, amazingly, lifted him in one smooth motion. Okay, where did that strength come from?

As I did so, he barked once, sharp and loud, in my ear, and I nearly lost my bladder. Those teeth could bite off half my skull.

The headlights swept over the road and over us. The revving engine announced it gaining speed. Couldn't he see my flashing lights? Then again, it could have been a she. Whatever.

I nearly fell when my foot slid out from under me, and the dog whimpered.

The headlights bore down on us and only then did I hear the laughter of many voices. A midnight joyride, probably with much drinking. The driver, I suspected, didn't have his eyes on the road. None of them did.

Jesus...

The truck didn't slow. Hell, it even seemed to veer *toward* us. I gasped.

The laughter turned to shouts. The squeal of brakes would certainly be the last thing I would ever hear...

I did the only thing I could think of, I dove forward with the dog in my arms. As I fell, I twisted my body and landed on my back, with the creature on top of me, shielding the dog from the ground. I landed hard, but it was the best I could do. The screeching truck stopped in the middle of the road, exactly over the spot the dog had been. And me, too. We would have both been dead.

"Dude, nice dog," said a bro from inside what turned out to be a pickup with an extreme lift. Other people inside laughed and peered out at me. The driver gunned it, and the truck shot off into the night.

The dog and I had ended up in the muddy ditch... and very nearly underneath my Jetta. I looked up at the creature in my arms, presently lying on my chest. He looked back at me, still panting. Still alive. Hot breaths pulsed at my neck. Warm blood spread through my flannel shirt. His tags jangled as I moved. I wondered what his name was. I also wondered who his owner was and what they would have to say about his injuries.

We lay that way for twenty more seconds, and, yeah, no way could I leave him here, not with those brown eyes so close to my face, and that drool hitting me square in the forehead.

And then it happened... the thing that broke through the darkness and self-hate, the thing that made me want to be a better me. A lick. A simple, small, tenuous lick, across my cheek. Then again, there was nothing small about that big tongue. But it had been a tentative gesture, a pleading gesture, and I heard it loud and clear.

"Let's get you some help, buddy."

After a number of attempts to stand, I finally did so. Somehow, I got him into the passenger's seat.

Gasping and dripping rain, I slipped out of my jacket and wrapped it around him. He filled the seat to capacity. Finally, I tucked in his big, bushy tail, gently shut the door, and dashed around to the driver's side and got in.

His head spilled over onto my lap while I drove. At one point, he gave me another long, dry lick over my wrist. But mostly he slept. And bled.

He needed a vet.

Now.

Chapter Two

Crestline had four vets, but none open at this hour. Redlands had a 24-hour emergency clinic. But Redlands was forty-five minutes away and down a steep and winding mountainside that I didn't entirely trust myself to navigate, even with my head clearing as much as it already had.

The dog whimpered. I whimpered too. I doubted the big fellow had long to live. He needed cleaning and closing and an IV drip…

Of course, I did know one other person who had once been quite adept at stitching incisions and sometimes even wounds. Someone who was presently sweating and anxious and still inebriated. A one-time talented dentist.

As I drove, I needed only to glance at the dying dog next to me to make my decision.

And floored it.

I took the narrow mountain turns much too fast.

The dog shifted, slid, and whimpered. I approached another car and did what any reasonable person would do under the circumstances: I promptly passed him in a no pass zone, and prayed like crazy another car wasn't waiting for me around the next bend.

There was.

A big rig.

I swerved hard, slammed the passenger side against the exposed rock of a cliff face. Stone and debris showered down on the roof of my car. The Jetta rebounded, and I managed to maintain control. The dog raised its massive, triangular head, then collapsed back down.

"Um, sorry about that."

On a straightaway, I gave the Jetta more gas. It growled and leaped forward. I like that in a car.

Moments later, the town of Crestline appeared in the windshield, the very town where I'd just had more than my share of alcohol. Maybe even more than two people's share. I knew this damned place like the back of my hand. I'd gone to school up here, found my wife up here, started my practice up here, lost my wife up here, and lost my practice up here. Oh, and I became a drunk up here, too.

I hung a right down Evergreen Road, now nearly empty at this hour. A small shopping center emerged to my right. At this later hour, the businesses would all be closed. One storefront, in particular, had been closed for many months:

Crestline Dental Care, Shaye Fox, DDS.

I drove around to the back of the dark building.

There, I parked near a communal dumpster, which I had shared with the other businesses, one of them being a popular ice cream shop. I'd often joked with the owner, a short man with a cone-shaped head, that his business gave me job security. He didn't find me very funny, and probably liked to see me go, if only to not hear my lame jokes anymore.

I checked on the dog. He continued breathing and panting, although listless. I dashed out of the car, through the rain, and over to my office's back door.

Mercifully, my key still worked. It had better. I still had tens of thousands of dollars of equipment inside here. My lease still had a few months left on it, and the center's management company hadn't let me out of it, despite the fact I wasn't working. It had become a really expensive storage unit until the lease ran out. The good news was, all my stuff was still here. The bad news was... despite my adrenaline fueled sensation of sobriety earlier, I remained inebriated.

I headed back to the car and over to the passenger side, slid my hands under the dog, and lifted him in my arms. Blood and rain water poured free from his fur.

He didn't whimper or move. *Uh oh.*

Cradling a massive, wounded dog, I hurried across the parking lot.

***

After twelve years in this place, I knew my way around even in the dark. Hell, I had slept in the waiting room often enough, back when the drinking began.

Now, I moved through the dark, knowing the electricity had long since been turned off. At the first patient room, I kicked aside a stool, shouldered away a medicine cabinet, and cleared a path to the dental chair, where I carefully eased the dog down into. He didn't make a sound, and I wondered if I'd lost him already. But no, not quite. His chest rose and fell, albeit barely. Thank God. Still, he'd lost a lot of blood. Hell, was *still* losing blood. My one-time office was going to look like a crime scene.

I grabbed some candles and a flashlight from the storage room. The locked medicine fridge still ran on battery power. With luck, the drugs therein would still be good. Mostly, I just needed to use a few CCs of anesthesia, alcohol and needle and sutures. Maybe some surgical drains.

With little time to spare, I went to work, first removing his collar with a metal tag, and something that appeared to be a leather harness of some sort. Next, I guessed his weight, found a vein, swabbed, and gave the big fella a shot of anesthetic. When he was clearly under, I cleaned the wound thoroughly with the alcohol, dislodging twigs, gravel, leaves and dirt. The poor guy must have dragged himself through the woods.

With the dog unconscious, I examined the wound before stitching him up. It looked completely illogical. I really had no explanation for it. Curious and horrified, I probed deeper, lifted the now-cleaned flesh, peering inside the stomach cavity. Surprised, I saw that the dog's stomach—that is, the organ itself—had been cut open with the same jagged incision. This would need stitching, too; and, later, once the dog had healed, these internal stitches would need to be removed by a real vet.

I bit my lip, wiped my brow, and stared down in alarm at my still shaking hands. Damn alcohol. The dog would die if I didn't do my best work—and from what I could tell, this dog deserved every opportunity to live. Sadly, he'd landed in my uncertain hands.

And so I spent the night repairing arteries, which I had never done, and minute stitching, which I had. I willed my hands to stay steady, and worked with the flashlight clamped firmly in my teeth, careful to avoid drooling into the dog's open wounds. I didn't know how to take his blood pressure, so I just went by visual vitals and, a few times, put my head down upon his gently rising chest and listened directly to his heartbeat. It remained slow but steady.

My initial shock became confusion—and then flat-out alarm—when I found several unexpected items *inside* the dog's stomach: a small packet of what I assumed to be cocaine... and a severed

human finger, partially digested.
    I stared at both, dumbfounded.
    What the actual fuck?

Chapter Three

While the dog recovered in the next room, I sat in my old office with the packet of cocaine, the severed finger, and an unopened twelve-ounce bottle of Jack Daniels in front of me.

I had kept the bottle stashed in the filing cabinet in a folder labeled Daniels, Jack. Interestingly enough, I thought about this bottle often over the past few months, hidden here in the office, its potential wasting away in a file drawer. Sure, the bottle didn't cost much, and I had purchased my fair share of them in the intervening months, but that wasn't the point. The point was, this had gone forgotten by everyone but me, remaining in the forefront of my thoughts, a minor obsession. Often, I wanted to get up in the middle of the night and reclaim this secret bottle, but to do so would acknowledge myself a hopeless drunk. By resisting, I felt I kept the disease at bay.

False reasoning, for in every other aspect of my life, the disease was alive and well. Spending ninety days in jail for having two consecutive DUIs was testament to that. Even attempting to drive home tonight proved just how out-of-control I was.

Like the dog, I, too, felt like I had been gutted and left for dead. Except I had done my own gutting. Of course, my wife leaving me for her boss hadn't helped. That's when the drinking had started. And with the drinking... and an endless procession of problems, culminating with me removing the wrong teeth from three different patients.

Yeah. Oops.

My insurance handled the malpractice lawsuits, but they, along with various government entities and lawyers, had collaborated to revoke my dentistry license. I had no one to blame but myself.

And, well, maybe my wife's boss.

Two helpless creatures, the dog and me. Both of us dying in our own ways. One of us brave as hell... and the other, well, the other was me.

Yes, he would have died tonight. No doubt about it. If not from his potentially fatal injuries, then from that out-of-control truck full of partying teenagers.

I thought of my work along his stomach lining, the meticulous stitching. I had cleaned the wound thoroughly. Penicillin would take care of any other possible infections. In due course, the stomach stitching would have to be removed, but only after the dog was sufficiently healed.

I thought of the stomach and looked again at its grisly contents before me.

The severed finger had turned brownish red, the flesh having been partially broken down from the dog's stomach acids. It was bent a little at both knuckles, and the skin at the base torn. White bone gleamed in the candlelight.

If I had to guess, wolfie here had bitten the finger clean off and swallowed it whole. Of course, the possibility existed that the big fellow had come across the severed digit and scarfed it up as surely as if it had been a Beggin' Strip. I doubted it though. Whoever had gutted this dog had also lost a finger in the process.

Good. Damn good.

I next looked at the open packet of cocaine. I'd already dipped my pinky into it, as they did in all the movies, and tasted it. The electric sizzle, followed by the almost instant numbing of my tongue, made it pretty clear this wasn't powdered sugar.

So, what the hell was going on? How did a dog end up with a packet of cocaine and a human finger in its sliced-open stomach?

I hadn't a clue.

I looked again at the bottle of Jack Daniels. Finding answers and seeing this dog through to health gave me a pretty good reason to not open the very bottle I'd been obsessing over for months.

I made a decision and headed to the closest sink. There, I unscrewed the cap, briefly smelled the aged contents with more longing than was probably healthy… and dumped the contents down the drain.

Against my better judgment—nothing new for me—I carried the dog from the patient room back to the front seat of my car. He was dead weight, still out cold.

On the way home, the sky lightening with the coming dawn, I stopped on a high cliff. There, at the edge of a rock overlook, I dumped the cocaine. I let the wind take the powder away, along with the empty bag. I next heaved the severed finger as far as I could out into the night, and watched it flip end over end until it disappeared, down, down…

Back in my car, I drove carefully home.

After all, I had precious cargo on board.

Chapter Four

The dog and I were in my mountain home.

I'd given him my bed, where he presently slept. Throughout the day, I periodically checked his bandages, made sure he was still breathing, and slept. Oh, and I wanted a drink so badly that I cursed God. Somehow, I powered through. Some-how, God did too.

Once at mid-day, fresh out of a nap that had done wonders to clear my head, I sat at my desk in my unused office and studied the dog's metal tag. Study was the operative word here, since I couldn't read the sucker. If I had to guess, I would guess it was written in Arabic, which puzzled me to no end. I mean, you look at a dog's tag, you expect to see "Fido" or "Spot" and a phone number, not the swooping calligraphy of Arabic... or something close to it.

More than the cocaine, the severed finger, or the

dog tag written in Arabic, my *reaction* to the dog intrigued me: the immediate interest I'd taken, and the powerful empathy I'd felt. Then again, it wasn't hard to be taken in by a creature who'd defied the odds to survive. A creature who had, undoubtedly, managed to escape some level of hell.

I browsed the web, clicking on page after page of dog breeds. I landed on a shepherd site, and followed the many links until I found an image that matched my dog. Well, not my dog... whatever.

He appeared to be an East Saharan shepherd— sometimes called a desert shepherd. I suppose that explained the Arabic writing, but that also would mean he hadn't been in the US too long. If he belonged to someone here, in the US of A, wouldn't they have gotten him English tags? If only so that if he were lost, others could read the information. Yes, more than likely.

I next Googled East Sahara and found it occupied a swath of land between Egypt and Eritrea, along the eastern side of the vast Saharan desert. Their primary language is Triundic, which I suppose the collar could have been written in. Like I would know. Then again, there appeared to be two different types of writing on the tag. Again, hard for me to say.

The web didn't have a whole lot of information about the dog breed, which had emerged a few centuries ago. Mostly, the breed had a reputation for their adaptation to desert life: their camel-like ability to travel long stretches without water, wide paws to traverse loose sand. They also sported long eyelashes and sealable nostrils. Going without water for sometimes up to a week was unheard of in the canine world, but not for this breed. Perhaps more than anything, the creatures supposedly had an almost supernatural ability to find their way home, even across the endless Sahara.

"Camels, homing pigeons… what can't this dog do?" I asked, automatically reaching for a beer that wasn't there, my hand grasping air.

I grumbled.

"Heal himself," I said. "He couldn't heal himself. I guess that's where I came in."

Desert shepherds herded everything from goats to sheep to camels, and were particularly valuable during long caravans, often playing guard duty as well. The breed also made fine service dogs, thanks in part to their unusual intelligence, hardiness and loyalty.

I thought about that. A guide dog? There had been that rigid harness I'd removed from him, but it hadn't looked like any guide dog's harness I'd ever seen. Then again, I didn't exactly know what passed for a guide dog harness in East Sahara.

Minutes later, unfortunately, I found a story about dogs being used as drug mules. The practice was common in… there it was. Common in the kingdom of East Sahara. According to the article, most dogs were destroyed upon arrival. Well, after the cocaine had been retrieved. They came via ship cargoes; amazingly, they also came with forged documentation.

"Crazy," I muttered, and reached again for empty air. I was gonna need to fill that space with a Diet Coke.

I switched off the computer, saddened and angry at humanity in general, and padded into my living room. A thick layer of dust covered the furniture I rarely used, and my coffee table held dozens of fast-food wrappers and empty beer bottles. Okay, that I did use. Drink coasters had long since been buried.

God, the place was a mess. Hardly a proper place for a recovering dog to stay, especially one that weighed over a hundred pounds.

And so, for the first time since the divorce, I started cleaning. And I cleaned throughout the day and well into the night. I often looked in on the sleeping dog in my bed, and I might have even caught myself smiling once or twice. Finally, at some ungodly hour, I collapsed on my living room couch with rubber gloves still on and the smell of Orange Pine Sol everywhere, surrounded by seven large, bulging Hefty trash bags.

Seven.

When I awoke the next morning, my empty stomach howled in protest. I couldn't remember the last time I'd grilled a steak or made a salad or did anything nice for myself. Mostly, I couldn't remember the last time I had cared about anyone or anything other than my next buzz.

But at six-thirty in the morning, I grilled the crap out of a suspicious-looking steak and chopped up a wilted head of lettuce. My salad dressing was a month past its prime but it would have to do.

The steak tasted damn good.

Fingers crossed it wouldn't give me dysentery.

Chapter Five

Crestline might be a small mountain community below Big Bear and Lake Arrowhead, but it sported not one but five full-time therapists. Cabin fever might just be real.

Now, I reclined in a plush leather chair... not quite a sofa, although it had the same relaxing effect. Dr. Manny Hernandez, a tall, quiet Cuban-American who seemed much too young to give advice to anyone, sat behind his desk parallel to me. I'd been visiting him weekly since the divorce.

He leaned forward at his desk, hands clasped before him, a position he seemed capable of holding for nearly the entire hour. Although oddly motion-less, he always appeared to be listening, and when he did speak, he did so in a quiet monotone.

"Tell me more about the dog," he intoned.

"It's an East Saharan shepherd, or the 'mini-camel' as some snobbish pedigree experts call it."

"Mini-camel?"

"Doesn't need much water, can travel vast distances across the desert. Supposedly has an innate compass akin to that of a homing pigeon."

"Fascinating. Tell me how the dog makes you feel."

I thought about that. "Alive."

"Why?"

I shrugged, my bare elbows rubbing over the leather. I looked up at the young Cuban silhouetted in shadows, framed by the big office window behind him. Sunlight flooded through the half-open blinds. Behind him was a great sea of pines. "He gives me purpose."

"Why?"

"He needs attention and help." I paused, wondering how much I should share, then shrugged. Technically, this was my hour, to do with as I wished. "After the divorce, my sister in Cleveland suggested I get a pet, and I resisted. I didn't want to bother looking after something living, especially when I wasn't properly concerned with looking after myself. Now, I can see the value of them. She will be happy to know that she was right… again." I smiled.

Dr. Manny said nothing. No other sounds disturbed the room, not the ticking of a clock or, say, the hum of a mini-refrigerator. Nothing. Only my breathing and the palpable thudding of my heart filling the silence. At least, filling it in my own head.

"Except I don't see him as an animal or even a pet," I said.

"You see him as a patient."

"Yes."

"And you haven't had a patient in a very long time."

I nodded. "I also feel a sort of… camaraderie with him."

"Because you saved his life."

"Yes."

"You feel responsible for him."

"In a way, yes."

I waited for the next question, but it didn't come. Out of the corner of my eye, I saw Dr. Manny casually bring his hands back together under his chin. Whether he meant to or not, he cracked one of his fingers. The *pop* resounded in the quiet room.

"I've only had him for two days," I said, "and he's done nothing but sleep, but somehow, he makes me want to be a better person. At least for now. Who knows what will happen when he's gone. I'll probably slip back into being the town drunk. Or who knows…" Except I couldn't finish my thought.

"Who knows what, Shaye?"

"Forget it. It's crazy."

"Who knows... you might keep him?"

"Yeah, that. Crazy, right?"

"No, Shaye. It's not crazy at all. No, not at all."

Chapter Six

The vet, Mike Tanner, looked grave.

"You'll need to leave him here for a few days." As he spoke, he stroked the dog's flank. The big fella didn't stir. Mike Tanner, an old high school acquaintance, had undoubtedly heard my sad story. Small town gossip and all that. "Stomach wounds are tricky and need to be treated with care. You did enough to save him, which is a credit to you, but I'll need to do some exploratory surgery and tie up any loose ends."

"A pun?"

He smiled. "The dog is severely anemic, Shaye. He desperately needs a blood transfusion; once done, he'll be up to his old tricks again in no time."

"Where do you get blood for a transfusion?"

"We have an in-house donor. A stray pit bull healing after neutering. The dog is healthy and has the same universal blood type as your dog."

"And what will happen to your donor?" I asked, which kind of surprised me. I'd turned into a big softy these past twelve hours.

"Ordinarily, he would be fostered out to get some socialization and training before the breed rescue screens people for his forever home, but I'm considering taking him home with me next week. Not like I need another dog, though." He chuckled.

"That's good of you."

"My wife might take a contrary view. So, what's the story behind this guy?"

I told him, minus the drinking and driving part, although he probably figured that out himself. When I finished, he nodded. "Yeah. I suspected this might have to do with drug smuggling. A detective friend of mine told me about it. The dogs are never meant to make it."

"But this one did," I said.

"Which says a lot about him."

I could only nod at that. "Where do they find the dogs?"

"Who knows? Could be from anywhere. Most likely, they pick up strays or steal them out of yards."

The huge dog lay sprawled on the table next to me, chest rising and falling evenly. Gravity pulled his lower lip down. His long white canines meant business. In fact, teeth that had completely bitten off a human finger.

"What do you make of this?' I asked, and fished out the unusual harness from my jacket pocket. "It was on the dog."

The vet took it from me, studied it, nodded. "A service dog's harness. Looks homemade, though. Or antique. Someone is really missing this dog, Shaye."

I thought about that. I also tried to wrap my brain around how someone could treat such a magnificent creature so poorly. Hell, *any* creature.

"If I need you, Shaye, I'll call. For now, get some rest. You look like shit."

"Gee, thanks."

Chapter Seven

The day after my visit with Mike, I found myself on a bench outside a lecture hall at Mountain Vista College in Big Bear.

I had been sober now for three straight days, a new record for me, post-divorce. As I sat, I kept my hands in my lap to stop the shaking. The big white dog was still with the vet. Mike informed me I could pick him up later today, and said he'd been making great progress. Oh, and that my stitching had saved his life. Yay, me.

I was nervous and excited to bring the dog home. And maybe a little scared too. He was a big sucker. What would be his disposition? And was I in any condition to look after him? Time would tell.

Students ambled past, most sporting backpacks and earbuds. Maybe it was a college of cyborgs. Certainly different than my days.

My mouth was dry. I needed a drink. I thought

of beer. Beer would do the trick. Oh, yes. But I could never stop at just one beer, could I? Nope. I needed to feel the buzz. And one beer wasn't enough to give me a buzz. One would be the beginning of a long procession of drinks that would take me far away from it all, into a land of blurry dreams, vomit, hangovers and court dates.

The lecture hall doors before me burst open, from which chattering students poured through, none of whom gave me a second glance. And why should they? They would go places in life, had friends and jobs and girlfriends and boyfriends. The pathetic man sitting alone on the bench was exactly what they hoped never to be. Even when I didn't drink, I looked like a drunk: unshaved, unkempt, unsteady. When the exiting students had slowed to a trickle, I stood on shaky legs and slipped inside the familiar classroom.

As usual, a half dozen students still milled about the popular instructor, all hoping to hear another one of his amazing life stories, as told by a man who had *lived*. I had once been such an admiring student. I knew the feeling, and I gave the students their time with him. When the professor looked up and spotted me behind the inner sanctum of revelers, he promptly and politely shooed them away.

"The prodigal son returns," he said, strolling over to where I stood.

"We live on the same mountain. I hardly went anywhere."

"And yet, I hadn't seen you for nearly a year."

I shrugged. "Life and shit."

"I heard about the shit, Shaye."

"I'm sure everyone has."

"You're not here to talk about the shit are you?"

I grinned. "A different shit show."

He nodded. "Let's talk in my office."

***

Professor Eli Haroun had lost his son fifteen years ago.

His son, a headstrong kid full of ideas to change the world, had joined a radical group and died in the streets of Palestine fighting for independence. Haroun had been devastated. That happened right about the time I first stepped into his History of Western Civilization class. The professor and I had recognized something in each other. I never knew my father and, after I'd graduated high school, my mother had moved back up north to be with her sick sister. I didn't want to move up north and stayed on the mountain, renting a room from a friend's family. My aunt and mother would die within years of each other, while I was in college, leaving me alone on this earth.

No surprise that I'd hit it off with the professor, who'd just lost his own son. Haroun had been there for me through thick and thin, from my graduation to my marriage, and even my divorce. Only recently, had I neglected him, but he was still there for me now. Like old times.

I brought him up to date on everything post-divorce… the DUIs, my time spent in jail and the loss of my dental practice… and the dog.

"We'll get to the dog, but first… you pulled the wrong teeth, Shaye?" said Eli. He shook his perfectly-shaped, bald head. "On three different patients?"

"That would be a yes."

He slapped his palm hard on his wooden desk and doubled over, his laughter reached a sort of subsonic quality to be heard only by the local wild dogs. I sat in a cushioned straight back chair and held its arms, chuckling along with him. Tears streamed from his eyes.

"Get it out of your system?" I asked after a few minutes.

"I think I pulled a back muscle," he said, sitting up. "My goodness, you are a hot mess, son."

"That about sums it up," I said.

He took in a few more breaths. "Well, did you bring the dog tag with you?"

The professor always had a way to cut to the chase. I produced the tag from a pocket and handed it to him. Short-sighted Haroun held it at arm's length, turning it this way and that, squinting.

"Eyes aren't what they used to be."

"I can see that." I wagged my eyebrows.

"Bad pun," he grumbled.

A few seconds later, he handed the tags back to me. "The tag is written in both Arabic and, I assume, Triundic, the local language of East Sahara, which I can't read. His name, in English, is War Daddy."

I blinked. Okay, the name felt right.

"Is that the literal translation?" I asked.

The professor nodded. "It's a reference to the *Arabian Nights*, one of the rarer stories. About a great warrior who is humbled by the gods and turned into a dog. But even in his canine state, his warrior's heart reveals itself. They called him 'War Daddy.'"

I felt a prickling on my neck. "They took the dog from his home. No doubt, stole him off the streets, tearing him away from his blind owner. Stuffed him full of drugs and shipped him to America, where he ended up in the San Bernardino Mountains, of all places. They gutted him to get their drugs, and he bit one of their goddamned fingers off and escaped into the night, dragging his own bloody carcass through the mud and rain. When I found him in the middle of the road, the dog virtually reassured *me* that everything was going to be okay."

We were silent for a minute or two.

"That," said Professor Haroun, "is a War Daddy, if ever I heard of one."

"Some dog," I said.

"Oh, and one other thing. There's a phone number on the collar."

***

We found the international calling code for East Sahara and Haroun placed the call from his office landline.

I rubbed my trembling hands. *How the hell am I going to ship a dog to East Sahara?* I didn't know, but there had to be a way. Even from where I sat, I could hear someone pick up. The professor spoke quickly in Arabic, paused, spoke again. Shortly, he hung up and sat back.

"What do you know about East Sahara?" he asked, a little too cryptically for my tastes.

"I did a little research last night," I said. "A mostly stable kingdom in northeastern Africa. East Sahara is predominantly Christian, just like its southern neighbor Eritrea. Triundic is the primary language, with Arabic a distant second."

"Stable enough, yes," said Haroun. "But they are currently dealing with insurgents, a radical group looking to overthrow the current monarchy. The country has suffered severe losses of late, mindless bombings of soft targets, anything to disrupt the country and turn the people against the rulers."

"What are you getting at?" I asked.

"The phone number on the dog tag didn't go to a home, Shaye. It went to a place called the Center of the Hearing and Sight Impaired. Or what's left of it."

"What do you mean?"

He sighed. "The Center was such a soft target. Much of the building had been destroyed, including their database."

"I'm still not following."

"The dog—War Daddy—had been part of a new governmental aid program to provide seeing eye dogs to the blind. Any and all information on the dog and its owner had been kept in their now-destroyed database."

"I take it that information wasn't on the cloud."

"Say again?"

"Never mind," I said. "What about paper work? Anything?"

"The program has been temporarily halted. There is nothing we can do."

"And there's no phone number on the dog collar for the owner?"

"It is a poor country, Shaye. Many do not own phones."

I drummed my fingers on the desk. "So what are you saying, then?"

"We do not know who owns the dog, and likely never will."

Crap. A part of me was overjoyed to hear this information, despite the tragic circumstances sur-rounding it. "Then I can keep him?"

"Do you *want* to keep him, Shaye?"

"I do, yes," I said. "Very much so."

Chapter Eight

A week and a half later, with the setting sun streaming brightly through the bay windows in the living room, what had been an extremely hot day came to a close.

I lived in a three-story log cabin home at the far end of an empty street. Read again: far end of an empty street. Yes, I had been called a recluse by more than one person. And maybe they were right. The house still felt new-ish to me... and far too big. Hell, it had a whole floor I barely went down to. That said, the back of my house faced the west, and had a nice, expansive deck from which I had the world's greatest view of the setting sun. At present, I stood in the kitchen, drinking a Diet Coke, watching the dog called War Daddy stick his nose into the house's every nook and cranny... including my nooks and crannies.

"Whoa, partner," I said, gently pushing his wet

nose away, again. I spilled some of my soda in the process. "Don't you know it's rude to stick your face in people's crotches?"

He was getting stronger, eating more. Today was his first full day without the dreaded cone. This morning, he had his external stitches removed. Without the cumbersome cone in his way, I noted he often sat like a big old lazy bear, up on his two front legs, right leg curled under him, left leg sticking out, ready to trip any unsuspecting passers-by. From this position, he could lick the jagged, red wound... and also his privates. Ideal indeed. Dog saliva, I would learn, contained antibacterial properties; licking his wound could help speed the healing process.

At the moment, he stood before me and looked at me oddly, as if I'd said a joke that he still puzzled over. He panted, his pink tongue hanging a few inches below his black gums. Mean-looking, vamp-iric canines pointed up like stalagmites from his lower jaw. He looked at me some more, then casually lowered his head and lapped up the spilled Diet Coke.

"Oh, that can't taste good," I said. "I mean, it's barely drinkable from the can."

A big, wet saliva splotch, about five times larger than the original spilled drink, shimmered in the slanting light of the setting sun.

"I'm going to need one of those orange caution cones that says, 'Slippery When Wet.'"

He flicked his gaze sideways at me, thick

eyebrows moving independently, seemingly with a mind of their own. He lowered his nose again, just in case he missed some of the soda. Dust stirred up by his sniffing scuttled across the floor.

"Knock yourself out," I said, and tipped more of the Diet Coke onto the floor. It splashed up onto my socks and even up onto the creature's white fur.

War Daddy looked at me, looked at the spilled drink, then trotted off into the adjoining living room.

"Oh, no you didn't," I said after him. "I give you half my Diet Coke and you turn your nose up at it? Your wet and very cold nose, I might add."

I had too much house, especially for a person living alone. The second floor alone had a dining room, living room, and a family room. The bottom floor had a game room, complete with a bar and pool table, another bathroom, and a kinda kitchenette. We'd gotten this place expecting a life together, kids, growing old here, retirement, the works.

I took a sip of the lukewarm soda and made a face.

"You're right," I said, and promptly got up and dumped the rest of the drink in the kitchen sink. Oddly enough, the *idea* of drinking a soda always appealed more than the *act* of drinking soda. I couldn't count the many cans of Diet Coke I found scattered throughout my house, barely touched. This never happened with the booze. Those, I drank. Then again, drinking Diet Coke never led to me losing my driver's license or my dental practice.

Sighing, I grabbed a hand towel and proceeded to clean the mess up—all while feeling watched. I looked up. Yup... big, brown all-seeing eyes took in my every move from just beyond the doorway into the living room.

"You want to help me with this?" I asked.

He didn't move. He was a big fellow, right at a hundred and fifty pounds. The muscles along his shoulders rippled nicely.

"You work out, boy?" I asked. "I should get back into shape myself. Lordy, it's been a long time since I've jogged. You like to jog?"

For a response, he got up carefully and moved over to the front door. There, he did what he had been doing for the past ten days: sat, and looked back at me. No, he didn't want to use the bathroom. For that, he went to the back door. Whenever I opened the front door, he trotted out to the edge of the yard, paused and looked back as if he wanted me to follow him. I never did, of course. I would call him back, and he would return, reluctantly. In fact, it grew harder and harder to get him back in. One of these days, I figured he would quit looking back... and just keep going. To where, I didn't know.

Maybe all the way back home.

East Sahara, I thought, *is a long, long, loooong ways from here.*

I didn't want him to run away. Already, I'd become a better person for having him. Not to mention, in short order, he'd become my best friend.

From the closed front door, he stared at me some more, then seemingly gave up. He circled once, twice, then curled up right there on the cold foyer floor. Air groaned from his nostrils in what might have been a sigh. He didn't sound happy. I didn't blame him. It didn't take a terribly observant person to see his discomfort.

"Your belly still hurts, doesn't it, boy?" Pain medication could only do so much. I suspected the wounds had to be excruciating, especially the interior ones.

I also suspected his wounds weren't the source of his agitation.

No, I knew the source. Anyone with eyes and a heart could tell.

"You want to go home, don't you, buddy?" I asked.

An eyebrow raised as if he'd understood me, which couldn't possibly be true. A moment later, he closed both eyes, and within seconds he'd fallen asleep. Yup, lots of pain meds. I watched the dog called War Daddy for a few more minutes, a dog built for the extremes of the desert, a dog who missed his home and owner. Very likely, his *blind* owner.

I turned my attention to the dishes in the sink, many of which hadn't been cleaned in weeks.

And lost myself in work.

Chapter Nine

I sat alone in my truck in the driveway.

Months ago, I'd backed it out of the garage and parked the Jetta in its place, figuring that a big dog owner needed a big dog truck.

Today had been rough. In fact, the entire last week was, too. War Daddy radiated unhappiness the way my ex-wife radiated scorn. The only difference being he didn't direct it at me as much as the situation. Seeing him miserable hit me where it hurt. I wanted him to be happy in his new home. With so much unhappiness, the urge to drink was overwhelming, to say the least. Better to fight it alone in the truck.

Wind thundered over the vehicle, rocking it gently. A pine branch scraping at the windshield caught my attention. It seemed to beckon me forward. Something else beckoned me, too. Something undeniable.

I sat up, turned the key, and backed out of the driveway...

***

A couple hours later, I sat in my living room drinking Budweiser straight from the bottle and watching War Daddy put on quite a show. For the past hour, he circled before the door, paced beneath windows, and put his forepaws up on the glass sliding door. Using my acute sense of deduction, I surmised that he wanted out. And not just to relieve himself.

A nearly empty case of Bud sat on the floor at my feet. I had gotten tired of getting up and going to the fridge. Cold beer was overrated. Beer was beer, especially if the goal was to get drunk. Unfortunately, the harder stuff tended to make me sick. So, I did it the long way. Beer after beer after beer...

I had bought three cases of the stuff. My only plan was to drink as much of it as possible before I passed out. As I drank, I ruminated...

I used to run a dental practice. Was even pretty good at it. I used to get up in the morning and go to work. I employed three hygienists. I worked on teeth, paid a lease, and consoled the fearful. I had been a pillar of society.

Now, I never received visitors and rarely even received phone calls. My friends had sided with my ex-wife, which made no sense to me. She cheated on me. I didn't do anything but get kicked in the metaphorical balls. Angry, depressed and filled with a quiet rage, I turned to drinking. The drinking, of course, became a problem.

The three people missing perfectly good teeth would agree. I would have chuckled if it wasn't so terrible.

What dentist shows up drunk at work? What dentist performed operations drunk?

Me, of course. Always me.

Just a disgraced ex-dentist. A forgotten ex-spouse.

I drank more beer as the night wore on.

War Daddy had been eating well. His wounds had healed nicely. Some of his weight had come back, and he looked strong. Damn strong.

Beast mode.

He circled again before the door, his claws clicking on the hardwood. I drank some more of the lukewarm beer. Lukewarm was good enough. Same buzz. My stomach shifted. I knew that shift. I would throw up soon. Sometimes I heaved, and sometimes I didn't when I drank. It's hit or miss with me.

To heave or not to heave, that was the question.

The dog was amazing to behold. He looked like a small polar bear with the confidence to match. Lord help anyone who went up against this beast. He continued pacing and stalking and trotting through the house as if he owned the place. He often paused and regarded me thoughtfully with those big brown eyes.

I finished the next beer, and the next, setting the

empty bottles on my pine coffee table. Keeping my eyes on the dog, I rooted around and found another bottle, wet and slick. I twisted the cap off like a pro and sat back in my leather sofa. The leather sofa made rude noises.

War Daddy paused, glanced at me.

"Wasn't me," I said.

His pink tongue lolling out of his mouth, he cocked his head to the side, one floppy ear hanging down. He would have looked cute as hell if he didn't make me feel self-conscious. I usually drank alone, after all. I shifted uncomfortably, tilted back the beer. God, it tasted awful. Maybe I needed to reassess my opinion of *cold* beer. I set the half-finished bottle on the coffee table, adding yet another ring to the wood.

And then it hit me. Or rather, hit my stomach.

Retching, I stumbled away from the couch and down a hallway, looking for a bathroom. My stomach lurched. I passed a spare bedroom. A family room. The laundry room. Where the fuck did I put the bathroom? I'd reached full drunk. Too damn hammered to remember the way to the bathroom. I stumbled some more, all the way to the end of the hallway. There, I pushed open a final door, found the porcelain bowl I so desperately needed, and heaved long and hard into it.

When done, I turned to see War Daddy watching me from the doorway.

God, I hated an audience. Even a dog. So much better to drink and puke alone.

I got up and made my way back to the living room, sat on the edge of the couch and thought of my ex-wife, my lost job, the pain in my stomach, the stench of my puke, the palpable loneliness that gripped me every day… and wept.

The weight on my knee was War Daddy resting his massive head. He didn't move, and, in fact, managed to make me smile, even if briefly. I leaned down and held that huge white rock and let him lick my ear while I ugly cried into his soft white fur.

Chapter Ten

"How are you doing, Shaye?" asked Dr. Hernandez, by way of getting our sessions started.

I started to speak, but stopped. How *was* I doing? I really didn't know. Still alone, lacking for human companionship. Still an ex-dentist and an ex-husband. Still thirty-eight, unemployed, listless, wayward. Still a recluse who lived at the end of an empty street.

But now I was something else, wasn't I? A dog owner? Did that not count for something, at least? I mean, sure, I remained all of those other things, but hadn't I become something a little more, too? Was it not honorable to own, feed, and care for a dog?

Oh, and I was now, technically, a recovering alcoholic.

Which gave me pause to wonder. Did I love War Daddy? Was it even possible to love a creature called 'War Daddy'? I certainly respected his tenacity, his verve, his will to live, a will to live which, I think, somehow radiated out to me, touched my life in a way that it had not been touched in a long time. The dog gave me a reason to get up in the morning. Gave me a reason not to drink. Even gave me a reason to, believe it or not, smile.

Finally, I answered, "Well, I haven't been doing good for a long time, doc. A really long time. You know that better than anyone."

He said nothing, nor did I expect him to. He tilted his head.

I raised my palms. "But now... well, now things haven't been so bad."

Dr. Hernandez shifted to the right, perhaps easing some weight off a buttock. I sat in the leather lounge chair across from him. My buttocks were doing just fine, thank you.

"Except... the dog is not happy. He's sad and listless, and that breaks my heart."

Dr. Hernandez actually sat forward at his desk. "Why is that?"

"He wants to go home, doc. He was a service dog. Bonded to his owner for life, no doubt. I'm sure he's heartbroken without her."

"How do you know it's a her?"

I shrugged. I didn't know. "It's just a hunch. Just came off the tongue. Could be wrong."

We sat there in silence some more. The clock ticked loudly, the only interruption of a profound silence. It kept on ticking, even as I got closer and closer to a decision...

***

The next two months were hard.

Hard because I knew the big guy wanted to go home. Hard, because I had grown to love him with all my heart. Hard, because I knew, deep down inside, he was not mine to keep, despite his being so far away from home. His pacing at the door never stopped, and grew more torturous to behold. The pleading in his eyes transcended simple dog and became positively anthropomorphic. Sure, maybe I read too much into it, but I couldn't deny his being miserable.

Sure he would play, and fetch, and roll around with me on the carpet. He played rough too, taking swipes at me with his huge paws, knocking me to the side like a rag doll. He never bit, although he bared his fangs and sometimes revealed his black gums.

After his final checkup, Dr. Mike Tanner declared War Daddy fully recovered. The dog was as strong as an ox… and growing stronger.

He had a nice big home with me here, with an entire mountain as his backyard. He didn't have to live in the desert or go days without water. He had comfort and food and water here. And he had a new owner who loved him so much. Yes, loved. Wow, so strange to say.

He could have run off at any time, but he didn't. Of course, running off wouldn't have gotten him any closer to home, and, I think, somehow, the dog knew that. The dog also knew that he needed my help to get home. Then again, I caught him rolling around on a dead snake the other day, so he couldn't have been *that* smart.

Yes, I had hoped this would be his new home.

But I think I had it pegged all wrong. This cabin would only be his *temporary* home.

I had looked into shipping the big fellow back to East Sahara. It was possible but super expensive. But then what? Who would pick him up? What would they do with him once 'they' got him? I didn't know, and I didn't like the idea of randomly shipping the big fella off to parts unknown. I had grown too close to him to do that. So close that I wept nightly thinking he might leave me... that he *must* leave me.

God, I had turned into a big softy.

At the end of the two months, with War Daddy still sitting by the front door, still pacing, still giving me that pleading look, I made a decision. And it was a helluva big one.

The washed-up dentist with nothing to live for might have just found his reason to live…

To return the dog home.

Wherever the hell that was.

Chapter Eleven

It had been one week since my "big decision" and the change in War Daddy was obvious. No longer did he sit by the window. Now he sat by me. No, he shadowed me, as if urging me along. As if to say: "Let's do this already!" It defied belief, but I could swear he understood what I said about trying to get him home. Hell, sometimes what I *thought*.

At present, he stared up at me, big tail wagging, kicking up dust everywhere. Drool hung off his lower lip.

"If I had a tail," I said, scooping wet dog food out of the can, "I'd be wagging it, too. Because, yeah, this is premium stuff. Only the best for fur face."

"Woof," he barked. His bark, amazingly, sounded almost exactly like that, at least to my ears. This was his conversational, inside-the-house bark. Outside, War Daddy's bark became positively thunderous and a bit frightening. A true battle cry. Those lungs could generate a wallop.

"Exactly. I would look silly with a tail."

"Woof woof."

"Okay, now you're just being mean."

I set the food down, and he attacked it. Literally.

My suitcase stood next to me. Just a single bag. It contained all the worldly belongings I cared to bring. I was surprised at how little I needed. To hell with everything else. To hell with my past and to hell with my ex. To hell with everything, that is, except War Daddy.

You are planning on coming back, right?

War Daddy continued chowing down, veritably inhaling the organic chicken chunks.

I'd spent the past week researching the country of East Sahara ad nauseam, reading anything and everything I could get my hands on. I learned much about this small kingdom in Northeastern Africa. For instance, unlike its rich neighbors, it was oil poor. Because of that, world events often over-looked the country. East Saharans were fiercely proud and hearty people. You had to be hearty when 98% of the country consisted of some of the most arid lands on earth. Apparently, their dogs were just as hearty or more so. I had living proof of that next to me.

Oh, and I'd bought one of those 'teach yourself courses' on Triundic. I would soon learn that my failed grades in high school Spanish hadn't been a fluke. I really was that bad with other languages.

Still, I spent every night with a headset on, listening to the CDs over and over, sounding them out with my fat, clumsy, awkward American tongue, learning a few words, butchering others, and forgetting everything else.

After dinner, in the living room, War Daddy came over and gave my protruding elbow a good lick, leaving behind a glistening gleam of saliva that matted down the hair on my arm.

"Good one," I said, wiping.

"Woof."

"Yes, I know. You've got more from where that came. You are a pretty impressive dog."

"Woof."

"Oh, you know that already, huh?"

I took a look at my home. My empty, lifeless home. It was dead to me, as it had been for the past year. In the back of my mind, I always knew War Daddy would never feel at home here. I knew without a shred of doubt I wasn't good enough for him. A better life waited for him out there somewhere. Not in here, with me.

"You ready to go home, boy?" I asked.

"Woof!"

"By the way, do you have any idea where home might be?"

He raised a furry eyebrow, cocked an ear at an unheard noise outside the kitchen window, flicked his gaze briefly at the sound, then settled it back on me. He shifted his front paws. Taut muscles rippled.

What a dog.

"Is that a maybe?"

We stared at each other in silence. Actually, he wasn't so silent. His panting filled the room. A puddle of drool already formed between his two massive front paws. The short, white fur along his stomach was doing its best to obscure his ragged new scar. Somehow, he knew we were leaving. I even suspected he knew I was taking him home.

"Look," I said, "I can get you into the country, but you're going to have to help me from that point on. They say that you desert shepherds have an uncanny knack for finding your way home."

"Woof."

"Glad to hear it, because I'm really going to need your help. I have no clue where we're going."

Pant, pant, pant.

I laughed and scratched between his ears. "I can't guarantee we'll find your home or your owner, but I'll do my best to take you as far as I can, wherever that might be. I won't give up if you don't give up, deal? By the way, don't you ever get sick of all that sand?"

"Woof."

I sighed and scanned my massive home, filled with expensive furniture, paintings and knickknacks collected from a life once shared.

"I'm a little scared, by the way," I said. "I've never done anything like this before." I paused, scratched under his furry chin. "And you know what the kicker is? There isn't a soul on earth who will miss me; maybe Professor Haroun, but not really. He has his own life. And certainly not my ex-wife; she's gone, baby, gone. It's just me and you, kiddo, and I'm going to find your home or die trying. Because I'm dying in here, in a way, and I'm doing no good to anyone, least of all myself. Maybe I can do some good for you. You're kinda worth it."

"Woof woof."

"Okay, now you're just getting cocky."

Chapter Twelve

On the way to the nearby March Air Reserve Base, nestled between Riverside, Moreno Valley, and the city of Perris, I stopped by Professor Eli Haroun's rustic cabin at the edge of a small town called Bluejay.

"Stay," I told War Daddy.

He jumped out.

"Good boy."

Shortly, we were inside the professor's home, which sported a fire in the fireplace and all the cozy feels that came with it. Outside, a light rain fell. Pictures of Haroun's new family covered just about every square inch of wall space. Smiling kids met my gaze no matter where I looked, dark eyes and white teeth. Many of the pictures showed Haroun and his wife, Avi. She was beautiful and exotic, and once, long ago, I had a serious and innocent crush on her. Hell, I still might.

"Would you like some tea, Shaye?" she asked, batting her eyes. Okay, maybe her eyes didn't actually bat, but they certainly blinked once or twice… in rapid succession.

"Um, sure," I said. Christ, still tongue-tied around her after all these years.

She smiled at me knowingly. Damn, somehow she knew about the crush, using some female instinct to uncover my innermost secrets. She left the room.

"You know," said Haroun, "someday, you are going to have to quit blushing around my wife. She might think you're smitten by her."

"I am, sort of."

"We know."

"That obvious?"

"To anyone with eyes and ears."

"Great. But it's just an innocent crush, you know."

"I know."

"I don't mean any harm."

He laughed heartily. "You've known her forever. If you haven't done any harm by now, then you never will."

Avi picked that moment to return with a tray of steaming mugs. "Shaye, you're blushing ear to ear. And I'm flattered. Crushes just don't go away. That's the beautiful thing about them."

I somehow turned even redder, if that was possible. "Can we, um, change the subject?"

They both laughed, and I regretted popping in.

But not really. After all, they represented my last connection to life here on the mountain.

You are planning on coming back, right?

"Too bad," said Haroun. "We were enjoying watching you squirm."

With the professor and his much younger wife sitting in big, over-sized wing chairs that faced the fireplace, I told them all about my decision to help the dog, my reasoning, my desperation, and my need to do something right in the world.

"Then coach Little League," said Haroun. "That is doing right, and you don't have to travel halfway around the world."

"Sounds dangerous," said Avi, looking at me sadly.

War Daddy arched an eyebrow and gazed at me as if to say: be strong, these are good people, but don't let them weaken your resolve.

I shrugged. "Yeah, it does sound dangerous. So, um, any last minute advice to keep me from, say, getting my head cut off?"

Haroun sat back in his chair as the fire crackled in the rock hearth. Rain pinged against the many windows, driven by gusts of wind. It was a good night to be among friends; also, my last night to be among friends.

You are planning on coming back, right?

"East Sahara is not for the faint of heart, Shaye. I suspect few foreigners visit the country. What's there to visit? A few old forts in the middle of nowhere?"

"A few old what?"

"Forts. I said forts."

Avi burst out laughing.

Haroun shook his head, sighing. "I'm surrounded by children. Remember, Shaye, alcohol is illegal. The country itself is fairly stable, although there are the grumblings of a revolution. Many are sick of the old ways and want to abolish the kingdom. Most are poor, and few even have a car. Camel and donkey are still the way to go. East Sahara has two fairly modern cities—the capital, El Alalim, and a somewhat smaller city Tel Hawah in the east, but that's it. The rest is rugged, rural, and fatal to those who don't know what they're doing. And some ninety percent of the country is open desert with nothing but nomads roaming it."

I nodded toward the dog. "He knows what he's doing."

Haroun sat forward. "You could die out there, Shaye."

"I'm dying here."

Avi patted my leg. "Then get a job, Shaye. Give this poor dog a proper home. Quit moping around and get your shit together."

I raised an eyebrow. "Tough love?"

"Yes. Is it working?"

"No. I tried all that. I don't know what else to do. Although coaching Little League does have some appeal." I looked at my former professor and his pretty wife with whom I'd had a crush on since I'd first met her. "But this isn't just about me. It's about him. War Daddy. He's special. He's been through a lot. He deserves a shot to go home. He deserves it so much that I'm willing to give it to him."

They sat silently. Outside, the wind and rain had picked up, now lashing the cabin.

Avi took my hand. "Then may blessings and luck be with you. Be respectful of the people, and they will respect you in return. You wouldn't happen to know, say, how to shoot a gun, would you?"

"A gun?"

"Well, you know, can you defend yourself?"

"I boxed a little in the Navy."

"Any good?"

"I was one and four."

"As in you won one and lost four?"

I nodded. Haroun laughed.

"Oh, Lord," said Avi.

"But the guy I beat was really, really big."

She rolled her eyes and might have murmured a little prayer for me.

Haroun jumped in. "Don't let him kid you, Avi dear. Shaye was a fencing champion in college."

"Just in my conference," I said.

"Fencing?" said Avi, blinking. "You mean with those skinny rubber swords?"

"They're not rubber," Haroun and I said together.

"Still. I don't see how waving one of those things around is going to help you."

I didn't either. Then again, I hadn't brought the

subject up either.

Haroun said, "You will be a stranger in a strange land. They are a proud people, steeped in history and tradition. How well you blend in, how well you understand, how well you assimilate, is entirely up to you. As for your safety…" Haroun shrugged. "They do not harbor terrorists and for the most part, they are a peace-loving people. Kidnappings are rare but there is an undercurrent of restlessness for the old ways."

Avi shook her head. "The restlessness has turned into much more, and there is talk of a civil war. As my father would say, just keep your nose clean and stay out of trouble. You are there to return the dog, not cause an international incident."

"Yes, the dog," said Haroun. "Stay with the dog. They will respect him more than they will you... at first. And the first chance you get, find yourself a gun."

I swallowed. "So when are these Little League tryouts?"

Chapter Thirteen

As a member of the Navy Ready Reserve, I can fly anywhere in the world for free.

The 'flying free' part isn't the key here, although saving a few thousand bucks is nothing to sniff at. No, the key here is that we would be landing at a U.S. military base (East Sahara is an American ally, a very loose ally, granted, but an ally, nonetheless) which meant no real customs. A major bonus when you're sneaking a 150-pound dog into a country.

You're really doing this….

Now, I sat in the hold of a massive DC-10, surrounded by dozens of pallets wrapped with clear plastic. As far as I could tell, the pallets were filled with medical supplies and food. Next to the pallets was a very large travel crate containing one very large East Saharan shepherd.

I'd remained on Ready Reserve because my

dentistry services were sometimes needed at bases around the world. As of yet, the Navy remained unaware that I'd lost my dental license. Of course, I hadn't volunteered the info and no one had asked. So, yeah...

I sat in an FAA-regulated fold-out seat, the kind you see the flight attendants drop down when a commercial plane is about to take off. I sat as close to War Daddy's crate as I could. For his part, he took this all in stride, lying on his stomach, his forepaws tucked under his chin. I noted the puddle of drool spreading before him.

"If there was a way to harness your drool into energy," I said, "we could solve the world's energy crisis."

His panting reassured me. Everything about him reassured me.

You're really doing this....

"By the way," I said to him, "you do realize that East Sahara has over one point three million square miles of desert, right?"

Ignoring me, he lifted a floppy ear at the barely perceptible change in the thrumming of the turbines.

"I hope you know where you're going, because that's a lot of desert, and wouldn't it be ironic that instead of drinking myself to death, I died of dehydration? Just give me something, Big Guy. Anything here, because I'm really beginning to think this might not be a very good idea."

He panted some more, and an eyebrow twitch- ed. Then, slowly, he lifted his lips and displayed his massive canines. The response seemed obvious: why fear anything when I have these?

"Good enough," I said. "I'll take it. One step at a time, right?"

The engine kicked into another gear, whining louder. I checked my seatbelt again for the tenth time. You've never traveled until you've traveled in the hold of a military cargo plane, lonely, dark— and definitely no peanuts served by flight attendants. Still, I reached into my jacket and pulled out a Snickers bar and some dog treats for War Daddy. I pushed a bone-shaped biscuit through the mesh. He scarfed it in a blink.

The plane shifted, and we started rolling. I'd officially started my journey to a small country called East Sahara.

Am I really doing this?

Yes... I am.

I wondered if East Sahara sold Snickers or if they had a 7-11. As the plane lifted off, War Daddy sank down into his cage, ears lying flat.

"It's okay, boy," I said. "You're going home."

Chapter Fourteen

Three hours into the trip, I was leaning up against the cage, reading a Robert B. Parker paperback in one hand and scratching War Daddy's head with the other.

He'd already thrown up a few times, and I had the great pleasure of cleaning it. At the moment, he appeared calm and relatively stable, albeit miserable. I left the cage door open, but he seemed content to stay inside and ride out the uneasiness and misery from within. I guess desert shepherds were not meant to fly.

Spenser was in the middle of cooking something fabulous for Hawk and Susan, while trading witty repartee with each other, when the plane's captain, a medium-sized guy with a head full of flaming red hair, appeared in the cargo hold. "Wanted to see how our two guests are doing. Don't get many passengers to East Sahara."

I thought of what Spenser would say, probably something irreverent and clever, mixed with a touch of social commentary, and settled for, "I'm taking him home." I pointed to the crate.

The captain came over and squatted next to the crate. "He's seen better days." He reached inside the crate and scratched War Daddy behind one of his miserably flattened ears. "We'll get you on the ground soon, poochie."

"He doesn't like to be called poochie."

"Really?"

"Actually, I don't like him being called poochie. Christ, look at him. A hundred and fifty pounds of muscle and slobber. Does he look like a poochie to you?"

The captain grinned. "You like this dog, don't you?"

"You could say that."

"How did you find him?"

"He found me. Long story. Let's just say he deserves a break."

The captain's red hair caught the overhead lights and appeared briefly on fire. War Daddy still lay on his side, tongue hanging out, drool splatting on the folded blanket inside the cage. Most of his fur had grown back, but the scar remained visible and red. "This dog was used to smuggle drugs."

It wasn't a question, but I nodded anyway.

"I've heard of this shit. A horde of bastards will sweep through a town at night and collect all the stray dogs and use them to smuggle their drugs around the world. Fucking pisses me off." He paused, breathing hard. "You found one alive."

I nodded. "He had a human finger in his stomach. I assume it belonged to the smuggler who force fed him."

"Poetic," said the captain. "You are returning him home?"

"I am."

"Guess it's not such a long story, after all."

I grinned. "I guess not."

"Well, good luck to the two of you. Do you know where he lives?"

"No, but I'm hoping he does."

"They say they're like homing pigeons."

"Let's hope. I don't want to die out there."

The captain reached his hand inside the cage again. His cheeks had turned bright red. He patted War Daddy on the head, and said, "One thing I know… stick with the dog. He won't let you down."

Chapter Fifteen

Nineteen hours later, just a hop, skip and jump away, the plane touched down at MacArthur Air Base, twenty-two miles outside of the capital city of El Alalim.

Upon stepping off the plane, I realized we had arrived at the wrong base. Apparently, the pilot had mistakenly flown us into hell itself. This transcended hot and went straight to whiskey-tango-foxtrot. I walked into a standing wall of 'screw this' so hot it could literally be life threatening. By the time we'd crossed the tarmac to check in with the staff sergeant on base, I'd sweat through my clothing. I'd also questioned my sanity once or twice. Or three times. I had no business in a place like this. None at all—

Welcome to East Sahara.

War Daddy stood next to me, looking from me to the sergeant, eyebrows lifting almost comically.

Noticing my reaction to the heat and genuinely worried about my physical welfare, the sergeant asked what my business was here. I told him I was here to return this dog home.

He grinned and said, "Nice knowing you."

Gee, thanks.

Not until after I'd stepped out of the admin office did I truly appreciate what I'd gotten myself into. Before me stretched nothing but sand and more sand… as far as the eye could see. War Daddy, I noted, looked east. I looked that way, too, and saw more sand. Shielding my eyes, I wondered what could be out there that constituted a home for a dog like this.

I'm about to find out…

War Daddy and I hitched a ride with three soldiers into El Alalim, since I would need a crap-ton of supplies, including camels. The dog seemed happy with this plan. As we drove, his tail wagged and the drool flowed without end. I jokingly said I understood why the breed could go so long without water—not hard to do when you can generate your own water supply. As we drove, he continually looked off toward the east.

Always to the east. Come to think of it, even at my cabin, he would look off toward the east. Which just so happened to be at my front door.

We arrived in town. The soldiers, who'd been caught up with War Daddy's story, wished me luck. I wished me luck too.

So there we stood, on a busy street corner in El

Alalim, East Sahara. Not a particularly inviting city. Dusty, hot, and the whole place smelled a bit like a barn. No surprise there, since piles of what I assumed to be camel crap lay scattered everywhere. The people here stared at me openly—many with blank expressions, and many more with suspicion. I could only imagine how out-of-place I looked. This wasn't exactly a tourist hotbed. I wanted a drink. A cold beer, in fact. In a country that prohibited the sale of alcohol, that wouldn't happen. Just as well. I needed a clear head.

I looked at War Daddy; he looked at me.

"Let's do this."

Chapter Sixteen

The low growl in War Daddy's throat ought to have been a warning, but my throat was parched.

At a cafe, I'd sucked down coffee, tea and water, but I needed something to take the edge off, and the offer stood right there in front of me.

"You want something a little harder. Whiskey maybe?" The wide, toothy grin that accompanied the whispered question struck me as contagious. I had no idea why War Daddy didn't seem as pleased as me. Maybe he just didn't like big smiles. The guy looked maybe twenty, and he'd been lounging just inside a narrow alley. Not an ominous alley, mind you. Merely another alley in a city filled with them.

I'd already had one stupid idea that I knew of—coming here in the first place—why not throw myself into another. "How much and where?"

"Follow me," he responded.

"You speak English well."

"Easier to sell to the American soldiers based nearby," he said, and winked.

"Ah," I said. "Of course."

His English was damned near perfect, which confused me. Had I known better, I would have thought we met at a street corner in San Diego. The kid had been to America, perhaps even lived there for some time. Yet here he stood, about as far away from the land of the free as possible. And here I stood, negotiating the purchase of booze like I'd gone to the inner city in search of heroin.

Anyway, I was about to commit to stupid idea number two and follow a black market smuggler to God only knew where in order to get my hands on a bottle of hooch or two. Maybe three? Who knew how long it would be before I could get another drink. I had no access to a secret file drawer with a bottle of Jack hidden away in it.

Though War Daddy's hackles had fluffed up and he moved forward with a great deal of reluctance, he didn't abandon me. We navigated several tight crevices in the alley until we arrived at a location that would have made a neat blanket fort for a nine-year-old, but was actually a small tent... a little cramped for the likes of War Daddy and myself.

"Wait here," said our guide. "I will bring you the whiskey. Do you have the money?"

"I want to see the whiskey first." I wasn't born yesterday. Truth was, I would have given a kidney for the booze. The young man didn't need to know that.

"Of course you do. I was just making sure you had the money before I bring the whiskey. It is very dangerous to be seen with it, you understand?"

"I do understand. You never told me how much." Amazing how stupid my craving for booze sometimes made me.

"One hundred American dollars," he replied.

"For a bottle of whiskey?"

"As I said, it is very dangerous to have it or sell it. Do you have the money?"

Even my craving protested that price, but then I thought about being out on the desert for God only knew how long, without alcohol. "Fine. Bring me two." I tried to sound cool, but even I could hear the desperation in my voice.

Though War Daddy had stopped growling, he still had his hackles up and was on edge. He leaned toward the guy with a look of clear menace in his eyes, straining against his leash.

"Relax, buddy," I spoke in a soothing tone after our guide slipped through a small hole in the back of the tent. My soothing tone was more for me than for the dog.

War Daddy looked back at me and locked his eyes upon mine for what seemed like a long moment, though it was probably only a second or two. That look, however, carried a strict admonition that I'd taken an unnecessary risk. He growled again, and turned toward the opening the young man had disappeared into.

I realized the opening just might have been the opening to the back of a truck, and the tent was a disguise. I had seen something like this in an Indiana Jones movie. Was this shit real? I'd only been in El Alalim a little over an hour and already I was going to get myself killed.

I had just thought that thought when two men appeared in the opening, guns drawn. Another man, God rest his soul, tried to slip a noose around War Daddy's neck. But the dog had already sprung forward, growling so deep that the sound seemed to come from everywhere at once.

My canine companion bit down on the man's forearm and twisted so hard that I think he broke the man's arm. Either that, or he yanked the arm out of its socket.

"Shoot him, not the dog,"

I flung myself at them... wrestling and grabbing for the weapons. Hands scratched my face, searching for my eyes. A gun went off. A second gun went off. War Daddy growled. The confined space spun around me. I hit my head on something hard, something metal. Blood poured over me. A man screamed—and abruptly went silent. No, not silent... he gurgled and fought for breath. I looked —holy sweet Jesus his throat was gone. Blood gushed to the pavement.

The third guy dashed off. War Daddy made to go after him, but I yelled for him to stop, and the dog did. Blood dripped from his jaws, where a scrap of flesh still dangled.

That did *not* happen. I didn't have... oh, my God, two dead guys lying at my feet.

I didn't know what to do. To call the authorities would mean explaining why I'd followed that guy into the tent in the first place. This felt like the kind of country where an American getting arrested would never be seen again. War Daddy would be destroyed, undoubtedly. But he did nothing but save my ass. And likely his own, too. What would those men have done with him? I didn't know, but they wanted War Daddy alive and me dead.

Shaking and nauseated, I knew I had to flee. I did my best to control my breathing listen. No running feet, no one shouting, or sirens wailing. The kidnappers/bootleggers/murderers had obviously taken me to a secluded section of town, perhaps where my own screams wouldn't be heard.

For now, no one appeared to notice or care what happened here... least of all to them.

Perhaps the guy who escaped would return shortly with more members of his gang.

Yeah, count on it.

And what, exactly, was in the hole at the back of the tent? Despite my nausea and fear, despite my need to get the hell out of here, an even stronger need gripped me. Did they really have booze?

I stepped cautiously through and into a dimly lit space. The opening didn't lead to the back of a truck. No, I'd entered an actual room. To my right, several barrels occupied a heavy shelf about waist high. Above was a shelf lined with several rows of bottles that appeared to be filled with what I assumed to be whiskey. Before I could take a closer look, though, the sound of scuffling came from behind me. War Daddy appeared in the opening, muzzle covered in blood. No surprise there. The dog needed to be washed stat.

And that's exactly what I did, cleaning the blood off the dog with the bottles of the good stuff. I paused often and drank from the bottles like a true wino. The blood poured off him, and when most of it was gone, I stuffed four more bottles into my duffel bag, and we got the hell out of there, stepping over the very dead bodies.

Chapter Seventeen

I'm not sure I would have ever found my way out of the labyrinthine alley system without War Daddy, but ten minutes later, we once again stood almost exactly where we had been when the man had approached us. What a difference twenty minutes makes. Wow.

War Daddy, still soaked and reeking of booze, led the way forward, and I followed. Behind us were two very dead men, along with bloody boot prints—my bloody boot prints. Perhaps I would do well to ditch these shoes. I did my best to not vomit, keeping myself together for the better part of thirty minutes as I searched for a marketplace. But at yet another alley, this one empty, I finally did heave until my stomach was empty. Then I heaved some more.

That done, I kept my head up and my eyes alert as we continued through the busy streets in search of some supplies. War Daddy attracted most of the attention, garnering smiles and nods from most of those we passed. It was as if I walked the streets with a minor celebrity.

After some inquiries in my halting Triundic, I soon found myself at a camel stable on the outskirts of town. From my research, I knew one didn't buy just one camel... but two camels. The second carried supplies. An hour later, and nearly two thousand dollars poorer, I was the proud owner of two shaggy camels, an old pistol, and a box of suspect bullets. I also bought enough provisions to last a month in the desert. God help me, but I hoped I wouldn't be out there for a month. The camel dealer gave me a crash course in how to feed the camels, saddle them, and, most importantly, how to mount and dismount them. I even bought new hiking shoes.

The camel trader pointed me in the direction of a small caravan that had set out earlier that day. On a map, he indicated their first stop, an oasis about twenty miles from here.

I thanked him and, with War Daddy in the lead, set off.

Just a man, two camels, and a dog.

It is said that War Daddy's breed can find their way home from anywhere. I was about to put that belief to the test.

***

The city streets disappeared behind us, and

soon, the bigger homes turned to shacks and lean-tos.

I led the two camels as a sea of sand opened before us. No, I hadn't a clue where we were going —perhaps that oasis on the map, perhaps not. I simply followed War Daddy out into the open desert.

What had happened back in the alley rattled me. Two dead men was a big deal. Yeah, I couldn't wait to get out of the city and into the desert. When we'd gone far enough out, I buried my old shoes. After all, the tread on them could connect to me to the killings.

Believe it or not, I enjoyed the walk... so far. The heat was tolerable. Or maybe I got used to it. I had dressed adequately, complete with long sleeves, cargo pants, and a wide-brimmed hat. Sunscreen covered my face and hands.

Visions of Clint Eastwood crossing the badlands in an old western crossed my mind. I even had to admit that I made that funny little sound from "The Good, The Bad and The Ugly" on several occasions. All in all, I felt pretty heroic for doing the right thing by attempting to return War Daddy to his home.

Maybe this isn't a stupid idea. Maybe.

Two hours later, my thoughts turned on me. What the hell was I thinking following a dog across the deserts of East Sahara? So stupid. Suicidal, really. I knew that with each step I took into the desert, my mountain cabin in Lake Arrowhead would drift further and further away. Like a mirage itself.

I took one last look behind us, at the shimmering dusty city at the edge of forever, sighed, and turned toward the unknown...

Chapter Eighteen

Walking over sand is easier said than done.

With each step forward, I took one back. It reminded me of the beaches at home, except these granules were dry, deep, and formed concentric waves for as far as the eye could see. The sand ranged from several dozen feet deep, to several hundred. Whole cities were sometimes found uncovered out here, particularly after strong sand storms. In essence, I surfed along upon an ocean of shifting sand, while the bedrock remained motion-less far below.

I found myself sweating at an alarming rate. Twice, I fell face-first. A half dozen times more I stumbled and fell to a knee. Like a living thing, the sand seemed to grab hold of my boots and hang on. The camels—and War Daddy, for that matter—moved gracefully, almost effortlessly, over the stuff.

I think I needed to wise up.

Time to hitch a ride. I'd been putting it off for reasons I didn't entirely know. Maybe I wanted to feel the Sahara for myself, to acknowledge it, to beat it. But I couldn't beat this stuff. Not with my narrow size elevens. Indeed, I wouldn't make it another five miles out here, let alone the twenty it would take to reach that first oasis... if that indeed was where we were headed. Lawrence of Arabia I was not.

With the lead camel already saddled, I did as I had been instructed. I gave the command for it to kneel, and he did so, begrudgingly. As the great creature propped up on what would be the equivalent of his elbows, I knew his willingness to allow me to ride upon him would be the difference between me surviving out here or not. Not that War Daddy needed me. The dog was single-minded and unwavering. The ease and flow by which his long, muscular form glided over the sand made it clear that I only slowed him down.

So, I did what any sane person would have done hours earlier: I stepped into the camel's sturdy saddle and took hold of the reins. As I did so, I gripped the high pommel, which jutted up like an F-150 gear shift. I gave the necessary command—a sort of whooping whistle—and the creature's rear end popped up. The sudden movement promptly launched me head over ass into the superheated sand. I lifted my face, spitting out gritty granules.

My second attempt had me leaning back more

and holding on tighter, and when the beast unfolded its long rear legs, I hung on and shouted for joy like an idiot. A small victory, yes, but one that just might ensure the success of this little adventure. Or, at least, delay my imminent death.

War Daddy watched all of this, panting and sitting on his rear haunches. His belly fur still hadn't fully grown over, but it was getting there. Even from up here, I could see his jagged scar, looking a bit like a lightning bolt. Apparently, I traveled with the Harry Potter of dogs.

I gave the reins some slack and heeled the big fellow just hard enough to get his attention... and then we were off. The second camel, tethered to the first, took up the rear. The three of us followed the great white dog eastward.

Ever eastward...

***

I sat high off the ground, higher than I expected.

I live in Southern California. It gets hot where I live, too, especially the deserts surrounding Crestline. But there's a difference between *driving* through a hot desert with the air conditioner on full blast while drinking an iced vanilla latte... and crossing the desert high atop a camel, with civilization and all its resources far behind you.

I could technically turn back now, and make it back to El Alalim long after dark. But that would mean abandoning War Daddy and his personal mission.

No, I thought. *I came this far, dammit. No turning back.*

Heat, wind, and sand soon became all I knew. That, and following War Daddy's half-mast bushy white tail, which curled up ever so slightly. The dog kicked up little sand and barely panted. I suspected he was in "energy and water conservation mode." Indeed, gone were the long globules of drool. The big fella would need that drool. Luckily, I had brought along four great tankards of water, all of which were strapped to the rear pack animal.

Oh, and I had my four bottles of booze, too. Shh.

Anyway, I seemed a natural at riding a camel. Go figure. Then again, once we got going, there wasn't much to do. Hell, I probably could have fallen asleep up here. War Daddy looked back often to see if we were keeping up with his fleet-footed pace. We were. His trot and the camels' natural gait synchronized.

Remarkably, by evening, with the sun setting behind us, we found the caravan. Or, more accurately, War Daddy found the oasis. Anyway, about sixty camels had encircled what could only be described as heaven on earth. An actual, honest-to-God oasis. Sitting right dab smack in the middle of the scorched earth.

After some surprisingly hostile stares, the East Saharan traders eventually warmed to War Daddy, the two camels, and myself—exactly in that order.

As I'd been recently taught, I watered and fed the animals before I watered and fed myself. With the two camels now sitting behind me, tethered to a stake already buried in the sand, the big white dog sat next to me, proud, larger than life, all eyes on him. He looked like a furry Sphinx.

I prepared food over a camel dung fire. That's right, I was cooking my food over dried-out, burning crap. My next closest neighbor, an East Saharan trader with a shock of wild black hair and kind eyes had offered the fuel. I thought that it was a helluva nice gesture since I hadn't thought of collecting feces along the way. Until I saw the trader only wanted to get close to my dog. Well, technically not my dog. Hell, maybe I was War Daddy's human. Anyway, he accepted the copious scratches and rubs with regal resolve.

I settled in with my dinner—lentil soup from a can, heated over the open dung fire—and read another Robert B. Parker novel by the flickering fire of burning poo. Ah, the good life. Nearby, the surprisingly large pool of water, shimmered in the setting sun. Truly a gift from the gods. Without it, there would be no life out here. As I read, Spenser and Boston seemed a long, long way from here, and that was alright by me.

I'd come here to help the dog, but already I was seeing the effects of leaving it all behind had on me... and I liked it.

You're coming back, right?

Except there was one thing I hadn't quite left

behind. Lying under the stars with a shimmering oasis before me, two camels behind me, and a dog next to me, I wanted a drink, dammit. I sighed and discreetly retrieved one of the bottles, unscrewed the cap, and poured three fingers into a metal cup. I sniffed the brownish liquid, wondering if it was safe to consume. Truth be told, I hadn't a clue what it had been made from or what might have been added to it.

With a suddenness that surprised me, I flipped the cup over and emptied the contents in the sand next to me. Lucky sand. My need for booze had nearly gotten War Daddy and I killed today. I considered dumping out all the bottles, but I didn't need to get crazy here. Knowing the bottles were near calmed my nerves.

More travelers arrived. Not surprisingly, the oasis was quite the happening place. Men laughed and gambled and played music. Their stringed instruments looked and sounded like nothing I'd heard or seen before. I would learn later they were called *oud*, a bit like a guitar on steroids.

Later, as the night wore on, I returned the Parker novel to my pack. Fishing around, I discovered something had been placed there, no doubt by the camel trader. When I pulled it free, I gazed at it with some surprise. It was a wooden flute. A block flute, I think it was called, with the mouth piece of one end.

Was it part of the merchant's gift package, so to speak? After all, he had packed the provisions for me, which I had thought had been damned nice. Then again, he had charged me an arm and leg for such materials. Either way, I found myself oddly touched and thankful... and curious about the small instrument. It reached inside me somehow, tugging at a distant memory that may or may not have been grounded in this reality; meaning, it almost seemed a past life memory, although I wasn't one to entertain such ideas.

No matter, though. I was not musical by nature —at least, I didn't think I was—although I'd attempted the guitar as a rebellious teen. Still, who was I to look a gift camel in the mouth? I wiped the mouthpiece off, and blew tentatively into it. The short, sharp note was immediate... and oddly satisfying. I blew into the flute again, testing the first of seven holes. Okay, that had a nice tone. I tested all of the holes, running my fingers quickly over them, landing them with an odd sense of precision. I tried different finger arrangements, and elicited melodious note combinations.

Wow, fun. And I seemed halfway good at it.

I paused, and noted my neighbors hadn't run for the hills—the sandy hills, mind you. Maybe I didn't sound too bad. Next, I tried sustaining a tune of my own, and I found a pattern that sounded nice to my ear.

Moments later, War Daddy lifted his big head and let loose with a long, plaintive howl that oddly accompanied my flute. Feeling a bit self-conscious, I lowered the flute, and War Daddy lowered his head, too. I wasn't sure if his howling was a compliment or not, although I was surprised to see many eyes on me when I pulled the flute away and looked around.

Again, I hadn't a clue if the stares were meant for me, War Daddy, or our duet. Maybe all of the above. I nodded at a neighbor, who smiled and nodded back. I slipped the flute back in the bag where I'd found it, oddly at peace and excited for the future. I wanted to keep playing that flute, but I wanted to learn without such a big audience in attendance.

I added more dung to the fire—oh, joy—and lay next to War Daddy. I stared up at the twinkling stars, and he stared at me. I wondered again if this was all a dream.

And soon fell fast asleep.

***

Come morning, I watched the sun rise over the eastern dunes and pinched myself all over again.

Others had already set out, and once I'd gathered and loaded my gear, War Daddy and I set off too. I rode high upon the lead camel, looking like a natural. And not at all like the has-been dentist I really was. War Daddy trotted happily ahead of me, across sand dunes that kinda looked like ocean waves tumbling toward a distant shore.

Soon, I fell into step with a wending caravan leaving the oasis, and heading in the same general direction as War Daddy. An honest-to-god caravan. Just a few months ago, I'd awakened from a night of hard drinking with a half-eaten chicken wing stuck to my forehead. An all-time low, even for me. Now... well, now look at me. I smiled.

At midday, the caravan came to a halt. I watched, perplexed, as the traders all hopped off their camels and proceeded to set up lean-tos, make-shift awnings and lightweight chairs. To my pleasant surprise, I discovered that such an awning and fold-out chair had been included in my supplies, too. I could have kissed the camel merchant.

Now relaxing in the hot shade, I drifted in and out of sleep. I dreamed of far off places and adventure. I even dreamed of a beautiful woman. I awakened with a smile. Two out of three wasn't bad.

Initially, I worried about the camels, but remembered they were perfectly adapted through millions of years of evolution to tolerate the heat and aridity of the climate. War Daddy was also specifically adapted to those harsh conditions, though he took advantage of the shade and sat next to me. Smart boy.

Hours later, with the sun marching to the west, the caravan picked up and moved on. I picked up and moved on too. With the others in the line following the camels before them, I followed War Daddy.

As evening approached, the winds and sand kicked up, and the caravan began angling north. As it did so, I sensed the big dog's agitation. He wanted to go east, I knew. But with night falling, it was best if we stayed with the caravan. At least, *I* thought it was best. As yet, I'd not stayed a night out here alone, nor was I eager to. Incredibly, I think War Daddy sensed my own nerves of leaving the safety of the group, and he gave me this night. But just this one night.

Later, after taking another go at the block flute, I drifted off into a deep, restful sleep. The deepest sleep I'd ever had. I might have been a desert nomad in a past life.

Not that I believe in that stuff.

Chapter Nineteen

At mid-morning, when the caravan angled invariably north, I saw the writing on the wall—or in the sand—and knew my time with them was short.

Indeed, as we crested a rise, War Daddy finally veered off. I veered off too, waving to my new friends. They nodded stoically and watched the crazy American venture alone into the biggest desert in the world.

"I sure hope you know where you're going, buddy," I said. "Because I sure as hell don't."

I had a map with my supplies, but what good would it do? My satellite phone, with its solar charge, was handy... but other than telling me where I was in the world, it did little use. It couldn't tell me where we were going, or how long it would take to get there. I did all I could do. I followed the dog. My personal DPS. Drooling Positioning System.

War Daddy, to his credit, moved confidently forward. His confidence gave me confidence. An hour later, after we had climbed yet another dune, I spotted my old caravan in the far distance, undulating over the hot earth like a great slow snake. I missed them already.

They would be the last people I would see for a long, long time.

***

The days piled up.

My immediate world consisted of nothing but waves of golden sand, clear blue skies, sweat, heat, wind, wagging tails, licks, snorting camels, sleeping under the stars, caring for the animals, and playing my flute.

A week past. Then ten days. Then I lost track of the days.

When you don't give a shit, it's easy to lose track of time. I had no desire to fetch the satellite phone buried deep in my gear. I had it for emergencies only. I had purchased it and the solar battery strip before the trip. The phone had worldwide coverage. The solar strip needed steady access to the sun. Um, not a problem out here. I would charge the phone if needed. For now, I lived as desert nomads had lived since time immemorial. On water, beef jerky and Cliff bars. To say I trusted War Daddy with my life was an understatement. And I was okay with that.

At some point, I began talking to the animals. I'd named the larger camel Jake (the camel I rode upon), and his smaller companion, Chester (the pack camel). Most days, the camels, myself, and War daddy had rather vigorous and sometimes heated conversations, although I tended to do most of the talking.

"Tell me something, you guys," I said. It was late evening, and I had a small fire going. I'd been wise enough to collect a plastic bag full of dried camel droppings back at the oasis; unfortunately, the camel dung was running low. Now there was a phrase I never thought I would say... or think. We needed another oasis, more water and dried turds. "Have any of you ever been cheated on? Oh, you were, Chester? Sorry to hear that."

War Daddy raised his big head from his big paws and looked at me. The dying firelight reflected in the dark pools of his eyes in such a way that I was pretty sure he understood every single word I said. Okay, maybe every other word.

"Sucks, doesn't it? Oh, you wouldn't know Jake? Lucky you."

I poked around the fire with one of the tent poles.

"I had it all, you know. A thriving dental practice, a beautiful house, nice cars, money in the bank. A lovely wife, as they say. You would think that would be enough, right? One day she was my wife... and the next day... gone. Just like that. I never saw the signs. I guess I was pretty busy. Not easy running your own dental practice." I looked at War Daddy. "I'm not sure where I went wrong. Are you?"

"Woof."

"Yeah, I think I took her for granted, too. It was easy, in those days, to put work first. Trust me, I learned my lesson."

"Woof woof."

"No, we never fought. And, yes, Chester, sex was good. I think. And get your mind out of the gutter, Jake."

That night, War Daddy rested his great shaggy head on my chest while I slept. And he remained in that position when I arose the next morning. We had slept on a simple blanket under the stars.

"Time to get up," I said. "We have places to go and sand dunes to see."

We made good time that morning and soon took our midday break. I played the block flute for my crew, and as my eyelids grew heavier with what was promising to be a helluva afternoon nap, I wondered again if this was all real.

Wind and pelting sand seemed to suggest that it was real enough.

That, and the camel snorting behind me.

At least, I hoped it was a snort.

***

Sometimes I found myself unable to look at War Daddy the same way, knowing those jaws and teeth had torn the throats out of two adult men. Was he a killer? He was, actually. But he had done so in self-defense. If not, I would have been dead. Get over it.

"Shoot him, not the dog," said the guy who had first beckoned us into the alley.

He spoke English, I thought. *Not just to me, but to the others.*

But why? The people of East Sahara spoke one of three languages, and none of them were English. And not just English. American English. Of all things, I'd run into an American gang of hooligans. But what did they want the dog for?

I didn't know, but I suddenly wanted to forget the bodies... and the fact that I had nearly been killed. After weeks of being sober, I no longer had the ability to resist the demonic voice of the bottles calling out to me from the pack. At least, that's what I believed. Hands shaking, I opened the side pouch where I'd kept the bottles hidden, drew one out, and didn't bother with a tin cup.

The moment the warm tingle of the liquid entered my throat, I knew I would finish the bottle. I'd fought it as long as I could, but some things were simply too powerful.

The buzz. It's all about the buzz. God, I loved the buzz.

I tried to ignore the pair of dark eyes with long, thick lashes gazing at me with what appeared to be sadness. Half way through the bottle, I glanced over again and realized he hadn't stopped watching me. Grr. And that's why I like to drink alone. Who needs to be judged, least of all by a dog?

I turned my back to the dog, and drank and drank...

And drank...

***

The excruciating light of the morning sun bored through my closed lids. No surprise I awoke with a massive headache. So far, I didn't have to vomit.

I pulled the blanket over my head to block out the light and tried to return to my stupor from the night before, but it wound up being futile because War Daddy had a schedule to keep up and he wouldn't allow me to make him fall behind.

Or so he thought. I was the boss of this little cavalcade.

"Beat it, Sir Drools-A-Lot. I'm sleeping in."

Within seconds of dozing off again, something long and wet painted the left side of my face with drool. Some of it got up my nose and in my mouth.

"So gross," I grumbled. "And did you get the memo? We're sleeping in today. As in, I'm not moving. Check that. I can't move."

Except my stomach chose this moment to lurch…

Oh, shit.

The vomit came long and hard. Somehow I had managed to miss my gear, although Chester might have gotten some backsplash. Chester has the worst luck.

Everything hurt and everything made my stomach churn up bile. By midday, I'd vomited so many times before that I understood why East Sahara had outlawed alcohol. It was too damned dangerous to drink it in the desert—or the stuff I'd gotten had gone bad. *Ack.*

In the late afternoon, with me riding high atop the camel and playing a merry tune on the block flute, we crested a particularly tall dune that overlooked a sprawling, vast basin of the most beautiful color I'd ever seen in all my life.

Green...

Best of all was the pool of shimmering blue water in the middle of it.

I nearly wept.

Chapter Twenty

This wasn't just an oasis, but a settlement.

Larger, wooden structures dotted the area, mixed with bigger tents that, I suspected, were permanent dwellings. There was a thriving trading post, complete with food and various wares for the traveler. I had no doubt that a sizable population lived here—hold up.

Was this War Daddy's home? Amazingly, dread filled me. I wasn't ready to say goodbye to the big oaf. Except...

Except it didn't feel right. I hadn't noticed any change in the dog's demeanor. No rushing headlong through camp. No additional excitement or eagerness.

No, this was just a stopover. I was sure of it.

I hoped it was.

I found a clear area near the east side of the oasis and unburdened my camels, then led my little adopted animal family to the water's edge and let them loose. The camels went in first, kicking up water, and dipping their muzzles in deep, taking long slogs of water, absorbing it like sponges. Hell, I could virtually see them swelling up. War Daddy lapped from the water's edge, like a proper dog, and when he was done lapping he jumped in with reckless abandon. Good boy!

He jumped in tight circles, turning and splashing and running.

"What is it that you seek?" asked a voice behind me.

Startled, I turned. I hadn't heard the old man approaching, probably because the big white dog was making such a racket.

"Pardon me?" I asked.

"I said your dog looks happy."

Except, of course, he *hadn't* said that. I frowned, unsettled.

"I hope so," I said cautiously. "And your English is very good."

"I'm glad to see all those years of education paid off." He came closer, shuffling down the slight incline to stand next to me. Rather than a staff, he leaned on what could only be called a tree branch. "Your dog wants you to play with him. You should."

The few teeth the man had seemed to point in different directions; indeed, his smile teetered on the verge of terrifying. He was graying and slight, back bent. He wore a common, flowing robe, tight on top and loose below, sandals on his weathered feet.

I opened my mouth to speak—no doubt to pro- test—but the stranger would have none of it. "Go on. Go on. He's waiting."

And so I did. War Daddy lunged at me, rising up out of the water like a great white shark. His forepaws hit me square in the shoulder and knocked me backward. I fell with a splash. He piled on top of me, leaving me sitting in the cool muddy water, which felt heavenly indeed. I needed this. The old man had been right. But War Daddy wasn't done with me yet. Oh, no. Not by a long shot. He pulled at my pants, dragging me deeper into the water; that is, until I found my footing and wrapped my arms around his muscular neck. We tumbled and rolled and splashed for God knows how long.

And all the while, the old man watched us from the sandy bank.

***

His name was Mahdi, and he insisted that we stay with him at his home.

It struck me that, once again, I was following a complete stranger down a narrow path toward something I wanted. In this case, an actual bed. Had I embarked on another stupid idea? I watched War Daddy's reaction to the man, remembering how he'd acted toward the smuggler back in El Alalim. The dog seemed at peace, so I relaxed a little bit, though I kept my guard.

We eventually arrived at a wooden structure between two palms, with a magnificent view of the oasis. A makeshift corral stood nearby for the camels to relax in, which they soon did. The home itself was one of the bigger ones, even if the roof looked questionable.

"Go inside and relax," the old man said. "I will care for your dog and camels."

Shouldering my gear, I kicked off my shoes and stepped inside. Okay, the place wasn't much, but compared to sleeping on sand for weeks on end, it might as well have been palatial. It sported a fire pit, a short table, two rocking chairs, and cushions along the wall. No electricity, but oil lamps hung from the ceiling, flickering softly. A wood burning stove—or dung burning stove—sat in one corner. At present, a pot was boiling on the burner. A short hall led to two bedrooms. Both sported actual beds with layers of heavenly blankets. Out back was a rickety outhouse. Next to that was a discreet shower nestled between two smaller palms and draped in animals hides. From what I gathered, a cord attached to a garden-variety watering can released the water from above. Jury-rigged or not, I imagined filling that sucker full of piping hot water and letting it sprinkle down around me.

Heaven.

I decided to try out the bed and its many blankets. It had more firmness than the bed I had at home, but it would do. I laughed at that; any bed would do, quite frankly. I wiggled my abused toes and listened to the gentle and soothing sounds the old man made tending to my animals.

Interestingly, my eyelids never felt heavier...

Chapter Twenty-one

The next morning, I awoke to the smell of bacon.

Heart aflutter, I hopped out of bed and slipped into his small kitchen, where Mahdi stood over the stove, working over a heavy skillet with a spatula. The sizzle unmistakable; the scent glorious. Bacon indeed.

"Good morning," I said in English.

"Good morning, my new friend. I trust you slept well."

"Very well. You have a very nice home."

"Nice is relative, but it is a happy place."

I couldn't agree more. I noted the paintings on the walls. The large vases in the corners. The rugs on the floor, the many blankets piled around the floors, serving as mats. Nothing electronic in the home, not even a radio.

Mahdi handed me a cup of hot tea. Ouch. Too

hot for me, though. He grinned as I set it aside to cool. Though I'd mostly been a recluse back home, talking to someone now was just what the doctor ordered... for my own mental health, quite frankly. My one-sided conversations with my animals was sounding suspiciously like crazy talk, even to my own ears.

"Thank you for the room," I said.

"It is nothing. It has been empty since... well, since the last traveler."

"How long ago was that?"

He paused over the stove, spatula dripping grease. "Ten years ago, maybe more, maybe less."

"It's been *ten years* since you've had a visitor here?"

"In my home, yes. Many have passed through Oroug Bani, of course."

"Well, I am honored," I said.

"No, my friend. I assure you, the honor is all mine."

He finished his work over the fire and came over to the table with two plates overflowing with crackling meat. He also brought over a cutting board piled with cheeses, nuts, dried fruit, and olives. I felt a bit like War Daddy, except I fought the drool that filled my mouth, whereas my old pal would just let it fall free. The difference between man and beast, I thought, as I bit into the crispy bacon. At least, I hoped it was bacon. On second thought it was probably goat or sheep. In rare situations, it would be camel. I really hoped it wasn't camel.

Mahdi asked about me, and I spoke between chewing and swallowing. I glossed over my failed marriage (and ignored the ugly bits about drinking and the malpractice lawsuit). Instead, I told him that I'd been a dentist, a lifelong dream of mine, but had taken time off for a little soul searching. *A lot of soul searching.* I mentioned finding War Daddy, and my desire to return him home, wherever home might be.

"You are here because of the dog?" he asked, raising his bushy eyebrows.

I nodded, biting down into the hard cheese. The fruit proved to be fresh figs, grapes and chopped apple. I was in heaven. Meanwhile, Mahdi ate slowly, favoring one side of his mouth.

"You are alone, then?" he asked.

"I have the dog," I said. "And the camels."

When we finished our meals, we sat on wooden stools along his front porch. Before us, children played on the shore of the oasis, building small muddy piles. To the south, I watched a small caravan crest and flow down toward the water. I could almost sense their eagerness. Laughter reached my ears from seemingly everywhere. Water was life. Laughter was life, too.

"Some say the dog finds you, not the other way around," said Mahdi suddenly, perhaps even randomly.

"You don't say?"

"Many call them angels. Others see them as a

good sign. Undoubtedly, you have been greeted with smiles everywhere you've gone?"

"Some have tried to take him," I added.

"Of that, I have no doubt, either. His breed is exceptionally strong. Some say as strong as the big cats… and, if provoked, as vicious."

I narrowed my eyes, catching a strange undercurrent here. "What are you saying, exactly?"

"The breed is a favorite in the world of dog fighting, Shaye. An unconquered hero."

I blinked at that. I had seen War Daddy in action. I had seen him, in fact, wage war on man… and win. Two dead men, two throats ripped out.

Mahdi waved off his own words. "But that is only if the dog is provoked."

We were silent for a minute or two. The three bootleggers had wanted War Daddy. Me, not so much. It had all been a set up to kill me and take the dog.

"The spirit in this one is very strong."

Of that I had no doubt.

I said, "Your wisdom tooth hurts you."

He nodded. "Perhaps I am not so wise, then."

"I have a small kit with me. I can look at your tooth. It's the least I could do."

The truth was, I had brought more than just a "small kit." The day before I left for East Sahara, I had returned to my practice and cleared out all my dental supplies; indeed, a very sizable bag rode upon Chester the Camel, the equivalent of a portable dentist's office. I'd had a hunch I would put it to good use.

When I had returned with my kit, which contained, among other supplies, a small flashlight and plenty of extra batteries, I said, "Okay, my friend. Open wide."

Chapter Twenty-two

He had an abscessed tooth, and a bad one at that.

I asked if he wanted me to pull it and he said no. I told him the only other option was a root canal, but to do so, I would need power for some of my equipment. He said electricity was not a problem, and led me to what turned out to be the village's sole generator. Shortly, amid great excitement among those who had gathered, I administered a local anesthesia to his mouth and jaw. When my new friend had become sufficiently numb, I fired up the drill... connected to the chugging generator and, after teaching the lad next to me how to use the portable high suction vacuuming unit (basically, all he had to do was vacuum up the blood, saliva and bits of tooth), I went to work. Hell, I even wore a mask like a real dentist.

An hour later, I had the abscess draining nicely.

The discharge was thick and disgusting. And necessary. That same discharge would have eventually poisoned the man's bloodstream and possibly killed him.

After further examination, I determined the abscess had drained completely. I next irrigated the canals gently with sodium hypochloride, cleaned out all debris, and filled the tooth with gutta-percha, a natural filling. Tomorrow, I would apply a crown to cover the whole thing. For now, Mahdi had been through enough. The crowd opened up, and I led the elderly man back to his home, with children and even a few adults trailing. I eased my friend into his bed of furs. He patted my cheek, thanked me profusely, and closed his eyes.

Back in my room, with War Daddy by my side, I fell into a deep and satisfied sleep.

***

Before I knew it, I'd built up a small clientele in the oasis village of Oroug Bani.

Over the next few days, my new "practice" had gone beyond the care of those who lived in the oasis and had extended to passing travelers. Despite War Daddy's restlessness, I spent the next seven days— working twelve-hour days—tending to everything from cavities to extractions. One guy had a bit of fish bone wedged up into his gums.

Mahdi made certain I had plenty of food and that my clothing was always clean, but he went well beyond that. He set up two assistants to help manage the traffic coming through the door of the "clinic," which consisted of a tattered lawn chair near the town's generator. I asked for donations from those who could pay. For those who couldn't, I worked for free. I gave all monies to Mahdi to distribute to my assistants and to the poor among us.

By the end of the week, War Daddy had taken to pacing the small hut we shared with Mahdi endlessly. I knew that pace. I had seen it in my mountain retreat. It would only be a matter of time before I knew the old boy would leave with or without me, and I couldn't allow the "without me" part.

And so, when I was certain I'd relieved the pain of all those near and far, I announced to Mahdi that I would be taking my leave soon. Once he realized he couldn't talk me into staying, he nodded and asked me to sit with him on his porch, as we often did together in the evenings after a long day of work. He packed his long, curved pipe with what I assumed was tobacco.

"Another dream?" I asked.

He nodded, lighting the bowl afire with a long match. There had been no shortage of his dreams during my time here, of which he enjoyed sharing with me. The man could give Nostradamus a run for his money. Indeed, he was considered the village holy man, and often led services in the small chapel just outside of town when the traveling preacher couldn't make it. Like many in Northern Africa,

East Saharans practiced Christianity, which, as far as I could tell, was differentiated only by their views of Christ. Apparently, East Saharans believed Christ had two natures: one divine, and one human. This was enough of a schism that they were forced to break away from the Catholic Church. A non-ceremonial religion would later be practiced by East Saharans, often in small chapels, led by local holy men with little pomp and circumstance. The places of worship were pillars in these small communities, helping the sick and feeding the poor. I liked that.

"Yes, Shaye, another dream."

"Did you see me jumping off a cliff again?"

"Not this time."

Yeah, his last dream had unnerved me. I told him *that* wasn't going to happen any time soon. He only shrugged and maybe whispered, "We'll see."

In just this last week, he had dreamed of leopards, a fighting ring, prison, betrayal. I asked where the pretty lady was, or the wonders of nature, or maybe a Starbucks or two? Oh, I nearly forgot about the explosion. Who dreams of an explosion?

"Okay, lay it on me."

"You will be pleased to know it is a woman, this time."

"Finally!" I said.

"She is a slave, I think. Certainly she is being held against her will. In my dream, you free her."

I winked. "Awfully nice of me."

"Shaye, the dog will lead you to her. And he will wait."

"What do you mean 'he will wait'?"

"Falling in love takes time."

"Whoa. Wait a second. Who said anything about falling in love? I haven't even met this woman!"

"Who said it is *you* falling in love?"

"It's not?"

Mahdi shrugged and winked. "There is more."

"Should I be worried?"

He ignored me. "The dog understands everything you say, Shaye."

"Er, say again."

Except he kept going. "The dog speaks too…"

I blinked. "No, the dog barks. What the hell are you smoking, Mahdi? And can I have some…"

"The dog speaks… you need only to listen…"

"Okay, that means absolutely nothing to me." Except… yes. Except I always suspected War Daddy knew what I was saying. In fact, I'd come to almost rely on it.

"He's just super smart…"

Mahdi grinned. "I can teach you to speak to him."

"I don't know how else to process what you're telling me."

"Then listen with your heart."

"I don't know what that means."

"You will. In time. Now, there is a cave—"

"Did you just say cave?"

"Yes, Shaye."

"Am I ever going to wake up from this dream?"

"Pray that you don't. This cave is not like any cave…"

"What… what does that mean, exactly?"

"It is a very special cave… a magical cave, some say."

"I need a drink."

He continued on... and told me all about the cave.

The magical cave.

***

The next morning, I bid the villagers farewell, and, with much fanfare which included hugs, deep bows and blessings upon me, we set out.

Four months ago, I had found myself staring dumbfounded at an empty beer case that I didn't remember drinking. But I had. The vomit was proof. Now I rode off toward the rising sun amid bright smiles, laughter, clean teeth, well wishes and real love.

I was with Mahdi. I never wanted to wake from this dream.

Chapter Twenty-three

The cave...

I'd found it that evening exactly where Mahdi said it would be.

Now, the reflection of firelight on the red walls created a frame around the rolling dunes of sand and more sand. The dunes appeared luminescent, like glowing hills upon the moon itself. Above, the dark-blue dome of the night sky reached down to the edge of the earth. Glistening stars of various sizes and intensities sparkled against the Stygian background.

I sat just inside the cave entrance with the fire at my back. War Daddy lay by my side, my protector as surely as the gun in my handbag. While I stared into the night—in particular, the wide ribbon of tightly clustered stars that made up the Milky Way —something happened to me. Was it the power of Mahdi's suggestion? I didn't know, but I suddenly felt... detached from my body... and connected with something bigger than me.

What was happening?

It all started the instant I entered the cave. To my eyes, it looked like any other cave... not that I'd been in many. But similar caves dotted the San Bernardino Mountains, of which I lived high upon. But this cave, in many ways, appeared almost too perfect. A smooth arched entrance that may or may not have been natural; an inviting, bowl-shaped interior with a level rock floor. The remains of what I imagined were decades if not centuries of fires in the center of the cave.

I'd tethered the camels a few dozen feet below, upon a mini plateau. From my position, I could see them huddled together in the moon and starlight. They appeared fine, watered, fed, relaxed. War Daddy sat next to me, looking out at the same view... at the heavenly light show above us.

The cave was perfect. The ideal cave. Cozy, comfortable, and I could envision making a life for myself here. Maybe hauling in some hand-made furniture and a simple bed and cooking supplies and never wanting for anything else ever again. But this cave didn't exist to be anyone's home. No, most certainly not. Not according to Mahdi, and I had started to believe him.

No, he'd told me the cave served as a transform-ative place, here for those ready, and invisible for those who hadn't yet seen inside themselves.

Wait, what? I had asked him.

And he repeated the words: *The cave was only there for those who were ready for more…*

More of what? I had asked.

More of life. More mystery, More love. More hope. More connection. More… everything.

It hadn't made much sense to me then, but it started to make sense to me now.

I felt both connected and disconnected to the world. Connected to something greater than me, but disconnected from all the problems, which now seemed small and few and easily solved. Drinking? Easy, just find a greater passion to focus on. Marriage problems? Easy, just find a new love. Loss of income and reputation? Easy, just start over. No friends? Easy, make new ones. A yearning for something greater, more meaningful? Easy, just follow your heart and the path will reveal itself.

These thoughts and more flooded to me, enveloped me, held me, soothed me, rocked me gently, and I sat there at the cave entrance and let them take hold, knowing I didn't have to do anything right now. Now was enough, being happy was enough. Sitting here within the heavenly glow of moonlight and starlight and reflective earthlight was enough. I was satisfied, and that was enough. I didn't need to think or work out my problems or to contemplate the divine or seek answers. I wanted nothing more than to bask and smile inwardly... and maybe outwardly too.

I sensed, yes, I sensed a connection to something more, even if that something turned out to be the part of me that had been buried by life itself, the part of me eager to rise to the surface now, the real me who hungered for love and life and light and joy, who loved to play and laugh and sing and dance. That part of me that I was meant to be, but had suffocated under some artificial drive for education, career, prestige, money.

No, not artificial. Such things were part of life, too.

An old part of life. I wanted something new.

But, for now, I didn't have to do a damn thing other than sit and bask and connect and forgive.

And maybe love again. Myself, this dog, this planet. Even my ex-wife. Okay, maybe that was going too far, but I had to let go of my hate for her. And find peace again.

Peace. Sweet peace...

***

Hours later...

I emerged from whatever spell the cave had cast over me. According to Mahdi, it was a tuning device. How it did that, I didn't know, but I suspected it had to do with something called ley lines, those vortices of energy that come together at certain points on the earth. And where these lines of energy criss-cross, well… miracles happen. Miracles like giving a drunk hope again.

War Daddy regarded me with his too-intelligent stare as he often did. His eyes reflected the heavenly light beyond the cave… and then some. In fact, they almost seemed too bright.

The Universe cares about you, Shaye. Cares more than you know. So much so it sent this one to help you.

A dog?

Would you have listened to anyone else?

A good point, surely. I scratched War Daddy's furry muzzle, and he leaned into my fingers. He both held the quality of occupying a lot of physical space, but also sitting so still that I sometimes forgot he was there.

As I hugged him, a young girl, maybe nine or ten with long black hair and rich olive skin, swam into my vision. She laughed and clapped her hands, and reached out for something... a harness attached to War Daddy. She laughed some more and hugged him around his thick neck. Together, they walked off down a dirt road…

I blinked, and seemed to awaken for the second time that night. Whoa, was that a… vision?

Wind swept over the cave opening, sprinkling sand within. War Daddy no longer lay beside me, but after a quick look around, I spotted him standing outside the cave opening. He gazed out into the night, fur rising and falling in the cool gusts. How much time had passed, I didn't know.

That's who he's come back for, I thought. *That kid needs him, not me, a full grown adult who had every opportunity to take care of himself. But a little girl.*

He needs to find her. And I need to get out of his damn way.

Mahdi's words came back to me then: *He will wait.*

I felt the tears, because I knew, perhaps stronger than ever, how much he missed his little girl.

Well, I thought, filled with sudden determination. *I won't make you wait a moment longer than you have to, my friend. Whatever it is we need to do, then let's do it.*

Apparently, it was to save a slave girl, according to Mahdi and his damn dreams.

The big dog looked back at me as a long stream of silver-tinged drool caught the surreal light beyond. As he gazed at me, words appeared in my mind:

"We've only just begun."

Okay, now why the hell did I think that?

Chapter Twenty-four

With breakfast eaten and everything cleaned up and packed, we set out again. War Daddy kept to a space-eating trot, which the camels matched easily with their long, gangly strides.

At midday, we stopped, and I set up the canopy as the sun passed over us at its highest point. The stillness around me was absolute, not a sound to be heard except the low whistling of the wind. Cascading sand made a noise, granules sprinkling over each other in some places, whole sections shifting in others. In essence, if I listened hard enough, I could hear the earth moving. The camels sat comfortably with each other, their heads together. I think Jake and Chester might be in love. Soon, we were moving again.

I thought often of my home and my patients. I tried not to think of beer. I thought of my ex-wife and her boss. I thought of my cabin and my Jetta and truck. I'd left much behind. I'd left an entire life behind.

Wasn't much of a life, I thought.

A hawk swept past overhead. The sight of them often surprised me and made me wonder where they came from and where they went. No doubt they "oasis hopped," if that was a thing. Though some of these rocky hills did have some signs of life, from scrub brushes to even rats, which I had seen once or twice. Except the rocky hills were few and far between.

The motion of the camel had long since become natural to me. Even when I sat at night near the fire, I caught myself swaying to the right and left. I came across no one during this time. Only me and my animals, although I never did consider War Daddy "mine." I merely borrowed him, leased him, enjoyed being with him while I could. Never had I seen a living creature, neither man nor animal, move with such determination, day after day. He kept his head high, his tail low, and the pace furious. We headed somewhere. To where, I still hadn't a clue.

As night fell again upon the desert, we found a dry *wadi* where we set up camp. When I say "we," it's really me doing all the heavy lifting. All three animals watched me curiously, awaiting their turns with water and food. I served myself last. I'd make for a fine nomad, I thought. The high walls of the *wadi* kept the wind out, giving us a welcome break as the night winds had been kicking up recently, bringing with them dust and stinging sand.

I lay back on my bedroll, looking up at the stars, and tried to remember who I had been, and decided I didn't like this game. Who I had been didn't much matter, did it? Who I had been had led me to being here, which I treasured. Perhaps I should have been terrified of the vastness of the desert. And I had been, a little. Okay, maybe a lot. But I started to get it. I learned how to survive out here, thanks to the help of the many people I had already met, and with the help of War Daddy, who had already led me to two oases.

The wind howled above, but not so much in this place of shadow and coolness. Except this place was home to scorpions and snakes. Luckily, I hadn't seen them yet, and I wasn't too worried. I had read that desert shepherds enjoyed eating both. Maybe the critters saw War Daddy and kept their distance.

By my estimates, we had been traveling for six weeks. Maybe longer, maybe less. Each night my sleep came deeper, more restful. Each night I dreamed of the dog and the desert and a small home at the edge of space and time, which I never quite understood. The home was really nothing more than a shack, and there I helped patients and animals, and, standing behind me, was always a woman, though I never got to see her face. I dreamed this dream often, and I reveled in it.

I watched the stars above, numerous and breath-taking. I listened to War Daddy's even breathing. The camels leaned in to each other at night, which I always found sort of... cute.

I should feel lonely, for never had I gone so many days without seeing another human being, but I didn't feel alone. Not with my animal friends, and the stars above. Not with the joy in my heart. Hard to feel lonely and happy at the same time.

Tonight, I lay directly on the sand, and the warm earth radiated up through my clothing and into my bones. Never had I felt so alive and happy and content. Never had I been so certain that I'd made the right choice. I didn't want to be anywhere but in this forgotten *wadi* at the far edge of the earth, with War Daddy by my side, and the two lovebird camels nearby too.

I entwined my hands behind my head, knuckles digging deep into the hard-packed earth, and smiled.

Chapter Twenty-five

The next day, I spotted a distant caravan in the north, and I couldn't have been more surprised when War Daddy suddenly angled toward it, especially considering we'd been going east all this time.

I shrugged and tugged Jake's reins, following the trotting dog.

Hours later, all eyes, of course, were on me and the big white dog. I heard much murmuring and *ooh*ing and *ah*ing. To his credit, War Daddy didn't seem to let it go to his shaggy head. In the midst of the friendlier faces, I spotted some shadier-acting characters, too… no doubt searching for the opportunity to relieve unwary travelers of the burden of their money or any other valuable possessions they might have.

Shortly after that, a large settlement appeared in a long valley below us, nestled along one of only two rivers that flowed through East Sahara, offshoots of the mighty Nile itself. Having studied the map I'd brought with me for hours on end, I figured we'd arrived at the city of Urwadi, a major hub of commerce in that region, although only about a third the size of El Alalim. As far as I could recall from the research I did before flying here, this city ranked third for size in the country, with Tel Hawah being second. A paved road even followed the river, and indeed, I could see cars and even buses below.

Heaving, bustling masses of people pouring into Urwadi absorbed the caravan. I was absorbed too. Though I didn't particularly enjoy throngs of people, it was nice to be among human beings again. I think. A cacophony of human and animal noises alike surrounded me: the rapid chatter of traders haggling over goods or hoping to lure potential customers; braying, barking and squawking chicken, goats, dogs and sheep. Oh, and the grunting of camels. So much grunting. All of which engulfed me as I rode high upon Jake through the marketplace in search of a space to settle in and rest.

Nearly a mile away, I found a grassy atoll along the riverbank, and went about the laborious process of setting up camp: unburdening the camels and rubbing them down, watering and feeding both creatures. Next, I watered and fed War Daddy, with some *scritches* between his floppy ears. For my efforts, I endured a slobbering unlike anything I'd ever endured. When I could see again, I arranged the canopy and chair just so, then watered and fed myself.

Though the sights and smells were quite distinct, one thing never changed: the behavior of people. It didn't matter if one reclined in a foldout chair in the deserts of East Sahara or sat on a bench in *The Mall of America*, people more or less all did the same things. They chatted, they laughed, they shopped, they begged, they talked too loudly, they looked happy, they looked miserable, they were alone, or they were in big groups. I watched it all flow past me from the little grassy hillock.

I felt sleep coming on, but I needed to re-stock my supplies, and one of East Sahara's biggest—if the not the biggest—marketplaces should do the trick. Still, I hesitated at leaving my camels and packs unattended. I briefly considered leaving War Daddy to guard the camp, but no way would I do that. The dog stayed with me, always.

I decided to risk it. I asked my local camp neighbor—a young guy with a young wife and new baby girl, themselves camped in something that looked like a mini-portable yurt, if he could watch my stuff for a few minutes while I shopped. He nodded and I mostly think he understood. On the other hand, I might have just as easily expressed to him that I was giving him all my stuff. I hoped everything remained here when I returned.

In truth, I didn't have much to steal. Just a few odds and ends, some food, clothing, my booze (which may or may not be poisoned). Obviously, I brought my money with me as well as the dog. What more did I need? Oh, and there was Jake and Chester, of course. Let's hope my new neighbors were as honest as their baby was cute.

With War Daddy on a rare leash, I ventured into the flowing crowd. As usual, the great white dog elicited stares and smiles. Children wanted to pet and play with him; I let them. More importantly, War Daddy let them. The dog seemed to be the people's mascot, of sorts. Their unofficial spirit animal. Maybe both.

What I figured would take only a few minutes stretched to almost thirty as the merchant and I haggled over the price of toothpaste and socks. Perhaps because he assumed a foreigner would be an easy all-around mark, he dug his heels in. But one didn't operate a dental practice without having a little business savvy… and so I dug in, too. We went back and forth as War Daddy sat between us, head turning, eyebrows raising alternately while the trader and I spoke beseechingly, defiantly, earnestly, pleadingly, angrily.

When the ordeal finally ended and each of us got what we wanted (although I figured I'd gotten the better end of the deal), I rushed as fast as I could back to camp, praying everything remained in order. Nothing made a crowd feel thicker than wanting to be somewhere in a hurry. When I finally returned to the spot I'd left everything, I breathed a sigh of relief. Everything looked as I'd left it. Chester and Jake chillaxed together like the lovers I suspected them to be, my packs sitting next to them, my small canopy intact. My bags… wait.

The zipper to my smaller one had been opened. Shit.

I scanned the area… there! I spotted a small boy slinking through the crowd, carrying my block flute. *The little shit.* He ran up to a man tending some camels, clearing and setting up his own camp. The adult remained clearly oblivious as the boy slipped the flute inside his robe, no doubt into an interior pocket. I glanced at my neighbor who should've been watching my things, and found him fast asleep on his blanket, head cloth pushed down over his eyes. His wife had gone inside the tent. Great.

I crossed the grass, even dashing through some encampments, and over to the kid and his father. War Daddy, I noted, dashed with me. The father heard us coming, glanced over his shoulder, saw War Daddy, and seemed about to smile in surprise… until he noticed the undoubtedly heated look in my eye.

When the father seemed to grasp that I was accusing his son of theft, he spun the boy around and spoke rapidly into the kid's face. The boy shook his head repeatedly, repeating the local word for no over and over. The father turned to me, motioned to his son, and shrugged, as if to declare the matter dealt with. I indicated he should search inside the kid's robe, and the man did, patting him down. Again he shrugged. Yeah, my case didn't hold. That is, until something clattered nearby. We all turned to see my wooden flute having fallen from between two nearby bags, presently settling on some flat river rocks.

The fury on the man's face was enough for me to start feeling bad for the kid. Eventually, the man turned to me, speaking rapidly enough that I was certain he couldn't possibly make sense to anyone. By this time, we had attracted a small crowd.

"I believe I can help," said a calm voice at my side.

I turned, surprised to see an older gentleman standing nearby... and speaking English, no less. "Wait..."

"Yes, Dr. Shaye. You extracted a tooth from me a few weeks ago. I am eternally thankful. And would like to show my appreciation with this... incident."

"How's your mouth?"

"Almost healed. Now, may I help?"

"Knock yourself out."

He nodded and spoke rapidly to the boy's father. I caught only a few words, but not enough to follow. The father answered with a few words I did not know, and the stranger turned back to me. "He says he is at your mercy. Please know, our laws are very clear concerning this sort of thing and the punishment is severe."

"How severe?"

"His son will publicly lose a hand."

"You've got to be kidding."

The crowd began murmuring around us. The old

man looked from them to me. "It is up to you, my friend. Do you wish to press charges? If so, I can fetch the town elders to carry out the punishment."

I swallowed. Though I certainly didn't appreciate the kid stealing my stuff, I obviously didn't want him to lose a hand over it. It was, after all, just a wooden flute that had been given to me, perhaps even mistakenly so.

I held up a hand and went over to the fallen flute. There, I examined it and shook my head. "My apologies, this is not my flute. Mine was, um, smaller with more holes."

"More holes?" asked the old man.

I pointed to the dimpled flute. "Mine had eight. This has only seven. Again, my mistake." The boy stood by his father's side, looking at me with both fear, incomprehension and defiance. I handed him the flute. "I believe this is yours. Just an unfortunate misunderstanding."

When the translator gave the man my response, the father clearly didn't buy it, but said no more and merely nodded. Undoubtedly, the boy would receive a private punishment (I hoped). But losing a hand seemed a bit much… and the father apparently agreed, despite his son's obvious guilt. He went along with the ruse, grabbed his son's ear, and hauled him away.

After they left and the crowd began to disperse, I thanked the translator.

"It was the least I could do," he responded. "You were very generous, my friend."

"Well, it was my mistake."

He winked. "Easy to miscount a hole or two. Let's hope the boy has learned a lesson…"

"And learns to play his new flute," I grumbled.

The man chuckled. He had a neatly trimmed beard, neatly manicured hands, and an immaculate white robe. None of which explained why War Daddy's hackles rose whenever he got too close. And so, he wisely stayed away. When something put War Daddy on edge, it put me on edge too. Indeed, upon second thought, the man oozed fake charm. Probably a schemer of one sort or another, and War Daddy had caught on early.

"My name is Ahmed."

He bowed and I bowed, too… awkwardly. He smiled and said maybe we would meet again, and as he left, he eyed my dog, who eyed him in return.

I shook my head at my new life.

You are coming home again, right?

Maybe. Then again, maybe I am home.

Chapter Twenty-six

Now flute-less, I sighed and headed toward my camp. On the way, I looked down at War Daddy. "At least one of us is happy. You never did like my playing."

Which was only half true. The few times I had played, I noted War Daddy had inched as far away from me as he could.

"Woof!" He smiled, or at least did something with his mouth that I took as such, then his ears flicked about.

"Well, I thought I was making progress. Unfortunately for you, my friend, I've taken a shine to the thing. I'll be on the lookout for another."

Except I seemed to have lost the dog's attention. Maybe War Daddy suffered a bit from A.D.D. For no particular reason, he veered to the right at the next street corner. I tried to pull him back with the leash, but wound up having my first lesson at water skiing—only without water or skis. Damn this dog was strong. My shoes slid for a bit before I gave up trying to make the dog halt and caught myself in a stumbling stride.

"Hey. This isn't the way back to camp," I said.

He didn't slow down. Maybe he recognized something and knew where he was? My thoughts returned to that little blind girl missing her dog. Maybe she lived around here. Okay, fine. Wow, I guess my trip's going to be quick and easy. Or at least quicker and easier than I expected. Hell, I'd been mentally preparing myself for another few months.

The narrow alley he led me down came to an end at a larger paved street where a few cars puttered by. Most of them were tiny and sounded like they had about as much power as a big lawn mower, nothing most Americans ever see. However, a black Mercedes SUV was parked about two blocks to my left. In this place, it practically looked like an alien spaceship from the future, even if it was a couple years old.

As far as I could see in both directions, on both sides, the streets held stores. The ones visible from where I stood at the alley mouth looked mostly like clothing shops, produce vendors, a bookstore, and a jewelry shop or two. Nothing at all that resembled a residence, though some of the stores probably had apartments above them. Didn't look like a great place to raise a blind girl, truth be known.

"So what gives, WD?" I said, scratching my

head.

Up ahead, three men wearing thawbs—those long white robes that most men in the city tended to wear—stood conspicuously still, two on the opposite side of the street from me, one on the same. The way they eyed their surroundings and had taken up positions made me think they're either undercover police, or up to no good.

War Daddy 'woofed' under his breath and stared down the street, but not quite at those men. He seemed to be fixated on the bookstore with the giant candle-shaped sign.

I opened my mouth to—for some stupid reason —ask the dog what was so important about the bookstore, but before I could say a word, a stunningly beautiful woman with long black hair and dark brown skin emerged from under the store sign, her attention absorbed by a thick, blue book in her hands.

War Daddy seemed to tense. "Easy, boy."

Hmm. Clearly, that woman could see, nor did she appear to be a little girl, more like late twenties. Maybe she was the girl's mother?

War Daddy tugged at the leash, dragging me across the street and onto the sidewalk, following her.

"Oh, come on. I've had quite enough of women in general. If you're trying to set me up—"

One of the men, who appeared not to be up to anything good, stopped leaning against the wall of a café and fell in step close behind her as soon as she passed him.

Shit. In shock, I glanced down at the dog.

The woman screamed.

I snapped my head up just as the book tumbled from her grip and hit the ground. The man had grabbed her from behind, hand over her mouth. Across the street, the lone dude hopped in the Mercedes. The second man on the same side as us ran over and grabbed the woman as well, fumbling with handcuffs.

"Umm." I squeezed the leash, not quite sure what to make of what my eyes told me. "Those are probably undercover cops, right?"

War Daddy emitted an urgent whine. The Mercedes swung a U-turn in the middle of the street, pulling up alongside the two men wrestling with the woman. Fierce as hell, she damn near got away from them.

The man with his hand over her mouth screamed and yanked his arm back, shaking his hand. She'd bitten him. She kicked and threw her head wildly... and caught sight of me. Her wide, terrified eyes narrowed.

"Help!" she screamed in English. "They're kidnap—"

His hand bloody, the man who she'd clearly bitten, slapped her hard.

I found myself running, with War Daddy leading the charge. No one else (all of about three people) on the street seemed to notice or care what was going on.

Right. Leave it to the dumbass American.

The second man shoved her face-first into the side of the Mercedes and the pair of them wrestled her into the handcuffs as another man inside opened the rear door.

They had a half-block lead, but I sprinted as hard as I could make my legs move. I was only slowing War Daddy down. Truth was, I feared for their lives if I let the big dog loose. I had seen what he was capable of first hand.

The two men shoved the woman into the back seat, still kicking and screaming—though not Hollywood style. She wasn't screaming in terror and flailing wildly… no, this woman shrieked in rage and tried to break bones.

"Hey!" I yelled, getting closer.

The woman twisted around and stared at me again; this time, the instant our eyes met, a surge of pleading, gratitude, and resolve passed between us. At the sight of me running toward them, she fought harder, trying to buy precious seconds.

The bitten man shouted something that translated into, "Shit. Go!"

His companion pulled a handgun from inside his billowing thawb, and pointed it at me.

Okay, maybe that translated to, "Kill him."

I skidded to a stop, hands up, but resumed walking toward them *real* slow, hoping they wouldn't risk the noise of a gunshot attracting too much attention. Maybe it came from watching TV, but something told me that men who kidnap random women off the street probably didn't want to attract attention. Then again, that same 'conventional wisdom' also said kidnappers tended to give up when the woman fought too hard… and this woman definitely fell into that category.

Someone inside the Mercedes pulled her the rest of the way in.

The man holding the gun on me flashed a wicked grin.

War Daddy plowed into me from behind and left, knocking me to the ground a split second before a gunshot rang out. My chest crashed into the pavement, blasting all the air out of my lungs and leaving me seeing spots.

Fortunately, the shooter hopped in the door as the Mercedes sped off, rather than shooting at me a second time. The woman's screaming cut off with a *whump* when the door closed. I cringed away from a blast of exhaust and dust, rolling around to sit. The windows had too much tint to see what went on inside, but I imagine it wasn't good.

War Daddy emitted a noise, part disappointed whine part irritated grumpf. Okay… umm. Did the dog know that woman would be abducted?

With a grunt, I forced myself to my feet and took off after the Mercedes on foot, shouting for someone to call the cops or help, or do something. Alas, I can't outrun a damn car on a mostly empty street… and this country evidently doesn't believe in license plates.

Despite the Mercedes vanishing around a corner

and not being there when I made the turn, I kept running for a block or two before collapsing against the side of a building, barely able to stand. Time (and the ground at my feet) blurred in and out for a few minutes.

"Wmf," said War Daddy, his mouth full.

I glanced up, still gasping for air.

He held a thick book, pale blue hardcover with gold trim, in his mouth… the same one the woman had dropped.

"No way." I plucked the book from his teeth, looking over the title, in Latin, *Oculus Intimus.* "Great. Just what I need. A constant reminder I was too slow to save a woman from being kidnapped."

The look he gave me felt like 'you went and screwed that up, now I have to do it the hard way.'

And yeah, I knew that sounded like a whole lot to infer from the way a dog looked at me, but somehow I *knew* he meant that. Just like he knew there was going to be trouble on the street.

I tapped the book cover. "You're that sure we'll see her again?"

"Woof!"

"All right. Fine. I'll hang onto this. I'm sure she'll want it back."

Chapter Twenty-seven

The sun had set, and I felt uneasy.

We still camped in the grassy park, and War Daddy, Jake, Chester and I had eaten our dinner. I sat back, my fingers laced behind my bed, looking up into the darkening sky and listening to the last of the merchants taking down their tables and tents, most storing them in the beds of trucks, but still others on wagons and backs of camels. Trying to relax proved nearly impossible. Hell, I didn't even know if I could sleep in the park overnight. But other traders were here, so to hell with it.

That woman had haunted my dreams. We only stared at each other for a few seconds, but my inability to stop her abduction grated on my nerves. I'd buried that book of hers deep in my bag so I didn't have to see it. The damn thing practically called me a chicken, or slow, or whatever. Nothing I wanted to deal with now.

I had just reached over to pet War Daddy, when the big fella tensed and sprung to his feet, looking out into the darkness with bared teeth and a deep-throated growl.

"What's out there, buddy?" I said, sitting up.

He stiffened, then slumped next to me. I jostled him, but he didn't move. Alarmed, I leaned closer and spotted a bright green fuzzy… Holy sweet Jesus, was that a… *dart* in his neck?

Many strong arms came from behind me, pinning my hands to my sides. The instant I opened my mouth to cry out, a rag smelling of ether covered my face and nose. I fought against the hands and rag, all while I quickly lost consciousness.

***

Odd sounds came to my ears, after which followed an awareness of an incredible headache and a terrible taste in my dry mouth.

As I became more conscious, sudden panic hit me. "War Daddy," I blurted, looking around in the dim light of what appeared to be a cold, stone room. I rushed to stand up, ready to charge into the darkness and find my dog—and camels—but soon discovered that my hands and feet were bound. I hit my head pretty hard on the cold floor when I fell.

"Tell Ahmed that he's awake," someone muttered in Triundic from inside the room, though I could see neither a speaker nor the person to whom he spoke. Thee words were easy enough to parcel out.

My eyes tried their best to penetrate through the shadows toward the sound of the voice, but they were simply unable.

"If you've hurt my dog," I said, "I'll kill you."

A quiet chuckle came from the shadows and then a metal object flew toward me, landed, and slid across the floor until it struck my leg. "You mean with this?"

I stared at my old revolver with the cylinder half opened and empty. Some good carrying a gun had done me. I fought my restraints again, and might have pulled a muscle in my shoulder. They had bound me pretty tight.

"Relax," the voice said. "Ahmed is just doing a favor for a friend. There is no need to be angry with him or any of us. It's just business, you understand?"

"What kind of business?" I hissed.

Another soft chuckle leaked from the shadows. "I am not privileged to know that information, but perhaps when Ahmed gets here, he will tell you."

The son of a bitch enjoyed this too damned much. I was thinking about what I would do to him if I could get my hands on him when the name 'Ahmed' finally registered in my brain. Could this the same Ahmed who had served as translator and gotten me out of the bad fix yesterday? It couldn't be, right? He and I had had a rapport with each other. Nah. No way it was the same guy.

My answer came soon enough. A few minutes later, the very man who had helped me yesterday emerged from the shadows.

"Dr. Shaye," he said, greeting me cheerfully. "I apologize for having to take such extreme measures, but you and your dog are very valuable to me and, well, I simply couldn't allow the two of you to slip away."

"You split-tongued bastard!" I spat. Though I hadn't really known the man, there had seemed to be common respect and trust established between us. Besides, I had fixed his damn teeth. Yeah, I did feel the bite of betrayal. "What have you done with War Daddy?"

"He is doing quite well. I'll take you to see him in a little while, if you can behave yourself."

"How am I supposed to believe a two-faced bastard like yourself?"

"I certainly understand the venom with which you are directing at me, Dr. Shaye. I can't say that I wouldn't feel the same way, but you have to understand two things."

"Just as long as you understand what a piece of shit you are."

"Now, now. There's no need for that." He chuckled. "First of all, I actually like and admire you. You have done a great service for me and I have already returned the favor, if you will recall. I do wish that our paths had separated afterward; however, the second part of what you must understand is another rather ugly circumstance that I simply can't ignore if I intend to stay alive and continue doing business in West Sahara."

"And what's that?"

"Someone in El Alalim is paying me a very high price to bring you and your dog to him. Who am I to turn down such an offer?"

"Who?" I demanded.

"He goes by many names. One of which is Sallah."

"Well, tell Sallah he can just piss off!"

Ahmed smiled sadly and exited the room. I fought, again and again, further damaging my shoulder, but so angry and frustrated that I didn't care.

Finally, I lay on the cold stone floor, gasping, as my unseen guard chuckled again. As I lay there, I thought of my old friend professor Ely Haroun. His claim that War Daddy would garner us enough respect to let us pass through the country was not entirely correct. No matter where we went, he did command attention, but in particular instances, the attention was not of a pleasant nature. I thought of the night I found War Daddy with his stomach ripped open and knew that at some point, I would come across the person responsible for this.

How I knew this, I didn't know.

But I knew it as surely as I knew I would get out of this mess.

Or so I hoped.

Chapter Twenty-eight

My captors held me in the same room/cell all night.

Soon after sunrise, armed men showed up, cut my legs free, and escorted me at the points of AK47s outside to a caravan, where I had a brief—and less-than-pleasant conversation with Ahmed.

"If you attempt to escape, you will most likely absorb a few dozen bullets." Ahmed flashed a smile as if he'd watched my son get a home run at Little League. "And, if you *do* manage to get away, you should know that caged dogs do not dodge bullets all that well."

I narrowed my eyes at him.

"Understand?"

As much as I didn't fancy the idea of being a prisoner, I couldn't simply abandon War Daddy to these bastards. It galled me, but I nodded. "Yeah."

They put me up onto my camel, which they'd

brought along, but left my hands tied. For some reason, they'd also left all my crap alone. Then again, in a country where they'd cut off the hand of a little boy for stealing a cheap wooden flute… they're probably just waiting for me to be dead. Then, it wouldn't be stealing.

So… out into the desert we rode, men with AK47s littered among the caravan, all giving me shifty looks like they really hoped I'd try something.

I'd been satisfied with War Daddy's treatment after having the opportunity to visit with him on the second day out of Urwadi. But seeing him in a cage only broke my heart, and made me all the more determined to set him free. We made eye contact, and the big fella actually wagged his tail. For no reason I could understand, I got the distinct impression he didn't mind what had happened. And crazy as it sounded, that he'd even expected it.

On the evening of the third day, we departed from the main trail and slipped back off into a deserted canyon. The red sandstone reminded me of the cave where I'd seen that beautiful portrait of nature. Were we near that formation? It really didn't matter. After all, where and how would I run?

As the sun began to set, we arrived in another canyon along with another winding caravan that, no doubt, included every form of smuggled goods imaginable. I learned from Ahmed that slaves were included, to be sold at an underground auction for the elites in El Alalim. In spite of my own problems, I couldn't help but think of the girl stuffed into the Mercedes SUV. Was she among them? I searched the faces as they passed me by and was about to convince myself that she couldn't be among them, when I saw her, and she saw me. I rode high upon my own camel, as did she. Both of us were bound. She stared at me blankly, sadly, shaking her head.

Throughout the evening after sunset, I noticed that a great deal of traffic continued to come in through the canyon, multiplying the population nearly tenfold. I could hear a great deal of commotion and occasionally, raucous outbursts of cheering from somewhere just outside our camp. I had no way of knowing what went on, but I figured I'd find out soon.

"Dr. Shaye," Ahmed said cheerfully, entering the tent where I had been unceremoniously tied to a stake in its center. "I would like to give you the opportunity to observe something that you might find very rewarding."

"The police have arrived?"

He chuckled. "I regret to inform you that the police have not arrived, nor will they ever. At least, not here in this God forsaken canyon. Anyway, I am afraid that I'll have to keep you bound and under guard, however. There are just too many opportunities for me to lose, shall we say, my greatest investment."

Two armed men came into the tent. One detached my chain from the stake while the other stood by to escort us out to whatever special activity Ahmed had planned. They led me outside the camp toward the sounds I heard earlier from a distance. As we approached, I began to get sick to my stomach, because I knew exactly what was taking place and what was about to take place. As badly as I wanted to refuse Ahmed's invitation, something inside of me would not allow me to turn away.

Four large bonfires stood around a stone pit with two tunnels on opposite ends and bleachers set up around them. On the bleachers, between 50 and 75 men passed money back and forth after having wagered on the last fight that had come to a bloody end. As I was led up onto the bleachers, I caught my first glimpse of the powerful white form of War Daddy in the pit. Around him lay the lifeless bodies of three large dogs with pools of blood around them. War Daddy himself was stained with the stuff across his chest and muzzle.

My hands were bound behind my back. A variety of weapons—guns and curved swords and knives—adorned just about everyone sitting in the makeshift, rickety bleachers. Some even wore sawed-off shotguns holstered like swords along their backs. I felt as though I had stepped onto the set of the latest *Mad Max* movie. At any rate, any foolish move on my part would surely result in death.

Still, I couldn't help crying out to War Daddy, who snapped his bloody muzzle around and spied me. I suspected he would have made an effort to lunge toward me, but wisely restrained himself. There were, after all, a half dozen assholes spread around the pit holding what appeared to be cattle prods.

A blast of yellow light erupted in my head as something blunt and hard ricocheted off my skull. I staggered and would have fallen if Ahmed hadn't held me up. If he'd noticed my outburst or the blow I'd just received, he gave no indication, which was, I suspected, an indicator of a true sociopath.

"You should be proud of your War Daddy, Dr. Shaye," Ahmed said, helping me find my feet again. The blow to my head was still smarting, and a distinct ringing in my ears persisted. "We have matched all sorts of dogs in the pit with him and he's made very short work of them all. In fact, the last bout was with three dogs, no less. They never even sank a tooth into him."

That he seemed so thrilled to have watched War Daddy slaying other dogs filled me with a kind of rage I had never felt before in my life. Had I not been bound and under guard, I would have killed him. Given my present circumstances, I said nothing. Rage and bile filled my throat.

"Are you familiar with jackals, Dr. Shaye?"

Still, I did not answer. Surely they wouldn't pit one of the wild dogs from the desert against him. In a few seconds, I found out that, no, they didn't plan to pit one of the wild dogs against him, but *three* of them. The moment the door of the tunnel opposite War Daddy flew open, I was torn between hiding my eyes and watching what happened.

In spite of wanting to puke, I couldn't help but feel a sense of awe for what took place in the pit in front of me. War Daddy had to be at least three times the size of each of the jackals. I assumed the smaller animals would have the advantage in quickness, but I was completely wrong.

War Daddy blurred into motion, taking the first jackal by the throat the instant they charged at him. He leaped into the air and over the top of the other two with the first still dangling from his massive jaws. When he dropped the lifeless form and turned back toward his attackers, they set upon him, but he knocked one aside with a strong blow and took the other in his jaws, blood spraying from the jackal's throat up into the crowd. The third had barely risen to attack anew when War Daddy leaped upon him and made very short work of him.

"Less than a minute!" Ahmed cried out over the roar of the crowd. "He has gone completely untouched again! I thought they might at least get a single bite or two in, but I was wrong." He reached into his pocket and eagerly paid a wager that he had made with another man nearby.

"That was amazing to watch, don't you think, Dr. Shaye?" he said as the evening came to an end and I was escorted back to my tent and re-chained to the stake.

I still did not reply, sickened by what they put my dog through.

As he and the guards left the tent, Ahmed

paused in the doorway and delivered the night's final blow. "I can hardly wait to see how he fares tomorrow against... the leopard."

Chapter Twenty-nine

Needless to say, I didn't sleep that night.

I vomited at least three times, the last, nothing but dry heaves. Though War Daddy had certainly shown himself to be indestructible, so far, I could not help but think of how a leopard was just one step down from a lion.

What have I done? What fate have I led War Daddy to? I saved his life and hoped to take him to his home, but instead, I have brought him to his death.

The following day, I refused my breakfast while I sat in quiet dejection. However, when the midday meal was brought to me, I realized starving myself to death was of little use to either myself or to War Daddy. As I approached the very edge of hopelessness, I couldn't help but recall the pathetic condition in which I'd found War Daddy—and how I had been in no condition whatsoever to help him, yet, he had survived. In the process, he had pulled me back from the edge. After my wife… I'd given up. On myself, on life, on the world.

Even if it kills me, I have to figure out a way to save him and set him free. And I'll need all my strength to do it.

And so, I ate my midday meal of almonds, figs and camel cheese and began to put together a plan. By the time the sun had set that evening, I'd put together what would surely top my list of stupid ideas and cost me my life... but with a little bit of luck, my sacrifice might buy War Daddy his freedom.

I'd once heard some baseball player say "luck just needs a little shove sometimes," and I decided that I'd put that idea to the test. I'd give luck a shove and see if fate, luck or whatever other cosmic force that had kept War Daddy and myself alive up until this point would do the rest.

Later, when my captors led me out in much the same manner as the night before, I gazed around at my surroundings. I took notice of where the camels had been gathered, tickled beyond all reason to see Jake and Chester. That I could actually discern my two camels from a herd spoke volumes to how much time I had spent with them, and just how far my life had taken me from my mountain home in southern California.

Clearing my head and trying to keep myself focused, I studied the terrain I would have to cover, the location of the other camps and the quickest route that would take me out of the canyon. I ignored Ahmed's banal chatter—which had a tone of excitement to it—keeping it tuned out and concentrating instead on the task that lay before me.

Once they led me up into the bleachers, I studied the fighting pit. No one, but no one, would expect me to do what I planned on doing.

Crazy, I thought. Just crazy.

The two gates into the pit looked like simple affairs: both opened by men who stood on top of metal mesh tunnels. At the far end of each tunnel sat various caged animals. One such cage indeed held an honest-to-God leopard. It paced and growled, muscles rippling, teeth bared. War Daddy sat quietly and panted in his cage. Did his tail actually just wag?

Only one factor made me believe my suicidal plan would work—the element of surprise.

Just as I hoped they would do, they first opened the gate on War Daddy's side of the tunnel, hailing him as the champion. He trotted down the enclosure, with the help of more cattle prods, growling all the way. I had a few things in mind to do with those assholes and their cattle prods. And yeah, it had to do with their assholes, too.

Okay, I thought. *Here goes nothing.*

I leaped to my feet. Ahmed whipped his head around and shouted something at me, but I'd already jumped down to the next row of seats, throwing my weight into one of the AK47-carrying thugs while grabbing with my bound hands at a giant knife in a sheath on his belt. He spilled over to the side, falling over several spectators. Knife in hand, I leaped from row to row among the heavily-armed men. Shouts—and the *ka-chook*—of pumping shotguns chased me. At the bottom of the bleachers, I jumped the last row in a vault that took me high over the wall of the pit itself. I hit the ground hard—on my hands and knees—and awkwardly enough to break an ankle, although I didn't.

A roar went up from the crowd; apparently, they wanted to watch blood spilled and didn't really care if it came from an animal or me. Obviously, the bastards had thought the vicious white dog would instantly rip out my throat.

War Daddy did indeed charge me. Except he didn't attack. Instead, he turned and stood guard over me as I found my feet while sawing at the rope around my wrists with the knife. Truly, I looked like a bumbling idiot—at least until the rope fell off.

By the time the crowd became aware that the dog wouldn't harm me, it was too late: I'd already reached the gate and with one swift, desperate kick, bashed it down. So far, so good. But as I turned to call War Daddy to me, the bloodthirsty bastards had released the leopard. Its long, loping, powerful striding figure raced down the second tunnel, visible past the mesh. At the far end, a second man opened the pit gate. The creature needed no prodding and seemed to be at full speed when it burst into the fighting pit.

That is, until War Daddy met the massive feline

head on, stopping it in its tracks. A deafening roar went up from the crowd as the two animals, equal in size and strength, became a cyclone of fur, claws and teeth—and I should know, since I stood in the first tunnel only a dozen feet away.

***

After the initial flurry of scratching and biting, the two animals circled each other, both growling so low and deep that the sounds seemed to emanate from the packed dirt of the arena itself.

War Daddy's fur stood on end near his tail, a phenomenon I hadn't seen until now, even when he'd battled the three jackals yesterday. War Daddy, I suspected, knew he was in the fight of his life. The leopard's fur rippled, its spots dancing and shimmering over tightly wound muscle. Its back was arched, not unlike a house cat. The leopard attacked next, swinging its left paw once, twice, and as War Daddy retreated, the leopard leaped forward, jaws wide open, aiming for War Daddy's neck. Had things gone the big cat's way, it would have smothered War Daddy, holding on tight, all while asphyxiating the big fella from behind.

War Daddy, however, had other plans. My furry pal met the massive feline in midair, and the two landed hard, rolling. The cat's back legs went to work, scratching in a blur, all in an effort to disembowel the desert shepherd. But, remarkably, the legs slowed their kicking, then they slowed more, and as the creatures rolled one more time, I saw why: War Daddy had the cat by the throat, and the tide had turned. My dog held that position for another beat or two and when the back legs finally stopped kicking, War Daddy released the leopard. The very dead leopard.

As the crowd erupted, something else erupted too: bursts of machine gun fire. There seemed to be something going on outside the makeshift arena.

With the crowd running in fear—and many of them randomly shooting weapons—I waved War Daddy into the tunnel.

"Come on, buddy," I said, keeping low. "Let's get the hell out of here."

Staggering from the wounds he'd suffered—the cat's back claws had done serious damage on his recently healed stomach—War Daddy followed me past the gate and down the tunnel. I desperately hoped I would be able to reach between the bars and unfasten the latch as I had on the gate leading into the pit, however, when I reached in and grabbed for it, I discovered it padlocked. The little bit of hope that had been there moments before dissipated.

War Daddy weakly trailed along behind me, collapsing with his head on foot, peering up at me. I could tell by the look in those large dark eyes, framed by those incredibly long, thick lashes, that he was in a great deal of pain. He counted on me to heal him once more and I had absolutely no way to do that right now.

Outside the tunnel, complete chaos continued:

shouting, screaming, gunfire, explosions and a cacophony of other noises difficult to identify from the mesh prison I found myself in. Still, I forced myself to block it all out and focus.

A firefight erupted right outside the gate, although I couldn't see who it involved. Not long afterward, a familiar, though very curious, face appeared in front of the gate: the father of the boy who stole the flute. He motioned for me to move back, and I did. Two shots later, and the lock was obliterated. He pushed open the door, and as I stepped through with a limping War Daddy, the man reached into his pocket and removed the flute.

I said thank you in Triundic. He smiled, bowed, and fled into the darkness, his debt to me apparently having been paid.

Meanwhile, hurrying didn't come easily to War Daddy with his extensive wounds. We moved cautiously toward where the camels had been kept, and I hoped that Jake, Chester and my packs were still there. I'd grown fairly fond of the snorting brutes, and couldn't bear the thought of them continuing in the company of Ahmed and his ilk.

Off to the left, I spotted more cages, except these didn't hold fighting dogs—they held people. Women! Instantly, I thought of the girl with the book. Hell, I'd been carrying the guilt of not being fast enough to help her for several days now, along with my guilt of leading War Daddy back to these bad men.

Although time was of the essence—especially

with the gunfire still erupting from behind me—I couldn't just leave *people* in cages. Running around in a ducking pose like I approached a running helicopter, I searched for something I could use to break open the padlocks. Many frightened faces stared at me and some begged for my help. The woman from the bookstore gripped the bars of her cage, staring at me. Though a note of fear did lurk in her eyes, she appeared more furious than frightened. Eventually, I stumbled across a man's lifeless body still clinging to an AK47. I pulled the weapon free, considered my options, then nodded. At the closest cage, I aimed for the lock, closed my eyes, and fired. A dozen women screamed at the same time.

When I looked down, the lock had disappeared, having either exploded into oblivion or having been flung far and wide. I pulled the gate open and gestured for the two women inside to leave, but they didn't.

Confused, I worked my way down the row of cages, shooting off the locks with War Daddy trailing behind. He no longer seemed to be interested in my protection, only in following me like a lost puppy. Or something hurt and dying. Okay, that thought made me extremely worried, but I pushed it aside as I worked at freeing the slaves.

Although I had freed nearly twenty women, none stepped out of their cages. Finally, I reached the woman I'd seen before, in the last cage of the row. She sat near the metal door, gripping the bars tight, her eyes wild with the most amazing spark. Who had a spark in their eye under such conditions? I asked her to back up. The instant she did, I promptly shot out the lock of her cage, a skill I'd gotten pretty good at.

When I pulled the door open, a subtle change came over her eyes—that odd way the people here have of smiling without moving their lips. "Better late than never," she said in halting English.

"Sorry. I'm kinda new here. People don't just grab women off the street like that where I'm from. Sorry for hesitating," I said.

"I know. And it's all right."

"We need to get out of here. Why aren't the others running?" I asked.

"To where? There is nothing but desert for many weeks in either direction. To live, they must stay here."

"Will you stay, too, then?" I asked.

"Of course not," she said. "I'm going with you."

I had just opened my mouth to protest, but froze at the sound of Ahmed's voice.

"I see that the old boy survived the leopard," he said casually. "That's an extraordinary dog. Now, before you do anything else stupid tonight, I have a pistol pointed at the back of your head, so I would advise you to toss that rifle aside and turn around slowly."

Reluctantly, I did as I was told, and turned to face Ahmed.

"Very good." He smiled, pointing my own

pistol at me. "I've lost a great deal of money tonight, but no matter. Once the dog heals, I will earn it back. It is you who I no longer need. I'm sorry, my friend, but this is goodbye."

Realizing that I was a dead man anyway, I did the only thing I could think of: charged the bastard. Head down, I ran at him trying to weave side to side. I saw a brilliant orange muzzle flash that preceded burning pain in my head—and then I saw nothing.

Nothing at all...

Chapter Thirty

Mahdi's crooked-toothed smile hovered over me.

Why it hovered over me, I hadn't a clue. In fact, it took many confused and frantic seconds for me to remember the fighting pit, the leopard, the slave girl, and Ahmed's final shot.

"Where am I?" I asked, certain I was hallucinating. Or dead.

"Relax," Mahdi said in a soothing voice, placing a hand on my chest. "It is too soon for you to move."

"Where's War Daddy? The kidnapped girl?"

"You mean *t*?" asked a voice as a familiar face hovered next to Mahdi's, the beautiful woman I hadn't been able to get out of my head ever since she disappeared into that Mercedes.

I tried to smile. "Yes. And War Daddy…" I began, but stopped short when his cold nose pushed up under my hand. I automatically scratched behind his ears. Though he didn't appear to be nearly as strong as normal, the glimmering spark remained in his eyes.

For a second I got the strangest feeling of contentment from him, along with an exasperated sense of fatigue... like he'd done something that should've been much easier, but had to go the hard route.

Since, again, that struck me as an awful lot to infer simply from making eye contact with a dog, I filed it away as a result of my overactive imagination.

Mahdi said, "He's been right here beside your bed the whole time. He hasn't moved, even to eat or drink."

"But he was wounded, and I was shot..."

The girl knelt next to me, her almond-shaped eyes alive and bright, her headscarf loose. "Do you want to hear the story or continue to try to guess what happened?" She had the unique ability to speak and laugh at the same time. As if the laughter formed the basis of her words. I knew it was a sound that I could grow to love. Her shocking fluency with English also surprised me, despite the strong accent.

"Point taken," I said. "Okay, hit me. Tell me what happened."

"As soon as you rushed the slave trader, your dog leaped through the air. Ahmed flinched, and the bullet only grazed your skull, knocking you unconscious."

"And Ahmed?" I asked, feeling around the bandage on my head.

"His throat was torn out."

"Mercy." I whistled.

"Apparently, we had arrived in the middle of an armed conflict between black market traders. Good for us, because we escaped amid the chaos." She paused, perhaps to ascertain that I was still cognizant. I nodded, and she smiled. "A curious man and a boy helped me get you up onto one of your own camels—apparently, the man recognized them. I sat behind you and held you from falling off. The boy and dog rode on a camel of their own. Your second camel trailed behind, still carrying your gear."

The thought of having her holding me, though it was completely out of place at the moment, struck me as being something that I wouldn't object to.

She continued her story, telling me how the three of them had traveled throughout the night and all the next day, and had arrived at an oasis very early the following morning. I had not regained consciousness, so they had all feared the worst, though I was still breathing and had a heartbeat. When they had arrived at a bustling oasis, the people living there recognized me right away and immediately brought me to Mahdi. It is then that the man and boy left. Apparently, the man was a big gambler, and had waged his life savings on the dog fights. He'd bet big on War Daddy and won a considerable amount of money. He was eager to repay the dog, if not me.

I kept silent for several moments after she'd finished speaking. War Daddy and I had certainly gone up and knocked on death's door and been able to walk away. No one was more surprised than me that my stupid idea had actually worked. Well, it had sort of worked. In reality, luck played the larger role in it all, though once I'd given it a shove, it certainly hadn't stopped working on our behalf.

"May I ask your name?"

"I am Ayda," she said. "And you are Shaye."

"I am very pleased to meet you."

She took my proffered hand, although, instead of shaking it as I expected, she wrapped her other hand around it as well and held it tight. "I am equally pleased to meet you, Dr. Shaye. Yes, Mahdi has told me much about you. You are a kind and giving man."

My face heated up, and I almost protested. After all, I hadn't given *that* much—just some time and dental expertise. And when it came to helping her, I'd hesitated too much when she needed me the most back at the Urwadi marketplace.

She sensed my need to protest and, seemingly, read my mind. "I do not blame you for hesitating to help me, doctor. You are a stranger in a strange land, and such things don't happen in the West. But you did not turn away."

"I hesitated," I said.

"Anyone would have in your place. Also, you didn't have to try to release all the slave girls, including me. You could have left us there. But you didn't."

I had done nothing more than shoot off locks, but I was too tired to protest any more. Besides, having someone think me heroic wasn't the worst feeling a guy like me, who had been down on his luck for oh so long, could hear.

Instead, I said, "I couldn't bear the thought of watching you get whisked away again."

"I'm glad you couldn't." She smiled. We sat quietly for a moment, smiling at each other. Eventually, she spoke, interrupting what had become a real moment for the two of us. "I do have a question to ask you."

"Go ahead."

"How did War Daddy get those horrible scratches on his belly and chest? He also appeared to have others on his body and some pretty severe tooth marks as well. To be honest, of the two of you, he was much more badly torn up and in much worse danger of losing his life."

Both Ayda and Mahdi sat spellbound as I recounted my stupid plan, and how it had instantly gone wrong, and how War Daddy had fought the leopard, and how everyone had scattered at the gunfire. I added how we had finally escaped the tunnel with the help of the father of the little thief.

She nodded. "Yes, it was they who helped us further. It appears the tide has turned. I believe it is you who now owes them a great debt."

"Ah, yes," Mahdi added. "Fate has a way of

appearing in the robes of those we least expect it."
He chuckled lightly and walked out of the very
same hut I had already grown to know so well.

I found myself looking up into Ayda's brown
eyes, and suspected that I'd gotten myself into the
kind of trouble that not even War Daddy could help
me with.

Next to me, a gleam flashed over the dog's eyes.

Or… did he *help* me get into this particular kind
of trouble?

Chapter Thirty-one

I spent many hours once again stitching War Daddy.

Mahdi supplied the thread and needle, which I boiled. Ayda and Mahdi both held War Daddy down, cradling his head, as I stitched as accurately as I could, pulling together the rendered flesh. Yes, it felt like deja vu all over again. This time, though, he had nearly a dozen such wounds, and many of them around his shoulder and back, too. The puncture wounds I could do nothing for, other than apply alcohol, which was again provided to me by Mahdi. The oasis might have been removed from civilization, but it was a favorite among the trade routes. That provided the benefit of some topical iodine antiseptic, which I used to clean his wounds. For his part, War Daddy only whimpered and licked his lips and Ayda's hands. Sometimes he shuddered uncontrollably, but still I stitched, and stitched…

***

By the time the dog and I were well on our way to recovery, the time I spent with Ayda felt like something bigger than either of us. Indeed, I could have stayed with her in that oasis for the rest of my life—and with War Daddy, of course.

Except this wasn't War Daddy's home, and I knew it. At the moment, the big fella was too weak to keep up his furious pace, which, though it pained me, I considered lucky. His need for rest gave me time to get to know Ayda... and what I learned I liked. A lot.

During this time, I happened across an old rapier among Mahdi supplies. He said he found it once in the desert and brought it home. Hadn't touched it since. The weapon felt good in my hand, well-balanced and finely made. No rust and a hardened, leather handle that felt natural in my hand.

Back in college, I'd been a conference fencing champion. It had been a nerdy sport, certainly not anything the chicks gravitated toward. It didn't necessarily have the same ring as "captain of the football team," but I had been proud of my accomplishments. I had worked hard to perfect the art, all of which incorporated age-old techniques. After all, fencing just might be the oldest sport of them all, having begun nearly five hundred years ago. As a skill, though, sword fighting was a throwback, and not very useful in today's modern age of weapons.

Still, it had proven to be damn good exercise... the footwork, the arm drills, the focus.

All of my training came rushing back to me on Mahdi's back porch, where I would spend the remainder of that day, with Ayda, Mahdi, and War Daddy watching me attack invisible opponents. I found it remarkable how fast the many moves returned to me, although I was far from tip-top shape, considering I was still healing from my own head wound. Still, it felt good to challenge myself, to move, to glide, to stretch, to once again summon the energy of the sport of champions.

"You are a man of many talents, Dr. Shaye," Ayda commented after many hours of this. I had long since ditched my shirt, and was sweating profusely. I knew I had attracted much attention to myself. I also knew that most Christian men in the region did not ditch their shirts. "You are a healer and, unless I miss my guess, one who has the ability to take a life as well."

"I don't really know about either of those statements," I said, stopping to take a break. Out of respect to her, I put my shirt back on "However, there is something that has been weighing pretty heavy on my mind concerning you."

"Then you must unburden yourself of it," she replied.

"How is it that you speak such good English?"

"My accent doesn't bother you?"

"It's, ah, very nice."

"Is it now?"

I could feel myself blushing. "Just answer the question, will ya?"

She laughed, a sweet sound. "I knew you would get around to that question eventually. I'm assuming that you haven't met many young women with dark skin like mine who speak proper English since you arrived in East Sahara?"

"A total of none." I couldn't help chuckling softly at her response.

"My father is the leader of, for lack of a better word, a nomadic tribe here in the deserts. When I was of age, he sent me to England to study. I actually hold a degree in art history." She laughed again when my eyes widened with surprise. "You are probably wondering why I was in Urwadi."

"You bought a book." I wiped a trickle of sweat from my brow before it could fall into my eye. "I saw you drop it."

"Not just any book—I'm chasing an old legend," she said, with a sorrowful sigh. "Anyway, as I've said, my people are nomads, Doctor Shaye. We had camped reasonably close to Urwadi, and I took the opportunity to visit the famous bookstore. Well, famous in these parts for its eclectic collection. I'm afraid the trip had proved to be a disaster."

I tilted my head. "Wouldn't your tribe be looking for you? Why didn't they show up at Ahmed's camp?"

Ayda gazed off into the distance with a look of grim resignation. "Because they had no idea where to even begin looking for me. I would not expect them to roam endlessly in search of a single blade of grass in the desert. It is not their way. We follow the tribe, not the other way around. I am certain my family believe I am still in Urwadi, reading my life away, as my father likes to say."

"Hmm." I wandered over to the pile of my stuff beside the tent and rummaged out that book she dropped the day of her abduction. Careful to keep it out of sight, I walked back over to her. "Chasing old legends, you say?"

She sighed. "Nothing I would expect a Westerner to believe in. I'm not sure I even believe it myself. I heard rumors of a book that contained a translation of some ancient passages that could be of use to my people. Assuming, of course, there is any truth whatsoever to the claims of mysticism." Ayda raked her hair away from her face, tucking it behind one hear. "Whatever good it may have done for my people is lost."

I flashed a rogue's grin and pulled the book out from behind me. "Oh, I don't know about *lost*. Gobbledygook maybe, but not lost."

"What?" she gasped and took it from me, flipping open a few pages, eyes wide. "It's not gobbledygook, it's Latin."

"Potato, po-tah-toh," I muttered.

She looked up from the book to squint at me. "Aren't you a doctor?"

"Dentist."

"Don't they make you learn Latin?"

"Only enough to pass the tests…" I whistled innocently. "Never could stand it."

Ayda snapped the book closed, staring at me with trembling eyes. "You really found it?"

"Technically, the dog did. But yeah. I had the strangest feeling I'd run into you again and thought you might want it back."

For a moment, Ayda seemed about to do more than smile, perhaps even hug me—or kiss me, either of which was fine by me; instead, she shifted herself away and promptly changed the subject. "So… Fencing? I remember watching the matches while I was in college. It was something I had thought of trying, but never seemed to find the time to do."

"I can teach you, if you like."

"Oh! I would like that very much. It would be a good skill to have."

"I'm not sure how useful—"

"Trust me, Doctor Shaye. Had I any weapon on me at all—and the skill to use it—those bastards in the street would have met their maker."

"Yikes."

She smiled sweetly. "Also, it looks like good exercise."

"It is."

"Then it is settled. When shall we begin."

I blinked, grinning. "No time like the present!"

I led her to the stump of a dead palm tree behind Mahdi's home. Admittedly, I was excited to spend more time with her and show her my skills, not to mention show off for her a little… and, well, be close to her. Yeah, I was smitten.

Of course, I'd never taught anyone how to fence, but teaching seemed to come naturally and she was a good student, eager to learn. I did the little things first: I adjusted her base, moving her feet with my own. Adjusting her hips this way and that, careful not to be too touchy-feely. Although a Christian country, Mahdi's curious neighbors were conservative to a fault. I did not want to ruin Ayda's reputation, or mine.

"Bend your knees slightly," I said, and handed her a short switch I'd found.

She put her hands on her hips. "A stick?"

"Sticks are safe, for now."

"Very well, give me the branch."

I grinned and did so. "Now align your feet with your shoulders. Good. Place one foot in front of the other to stabilize yourself. Good, good. This is your base, it must be strong, but you must learn to move out of it as well."

I noticed many eyes on us, so I kept a proper space between us. She had dressed in a long robe, but the strong breeze made it rather obvious a curvy body lay hidden beneath.

I swallowed. "Loosen yourself up," I said with a bit of a cough, shaking off the image of her fine figure. "You're too stiff."

"This isn't exactly a natural position for me," she replied, laughing. Indeed, she wavered, nearly losing her balance.

All kinds of strange thoughts swirled through

my head after that response, and I forced myself back into focus. This would not be easy. Already, a strong chemistry had formed between us, and her shapely form made it difficult to concentrate on anything else.

Focus, Shaye.

I took my place next to her, adopting a similar on-guard pose. "Now, follow my movements."

She nodded, and I demonstrated the first of a series of beginning moves, once again surprised at how easily all of this had come back to me after, what, nearly a decade?

I couldn't exactly call her a natural at fencing, though she had more than enough grace and dexterity for it. Soon, we flowed together, like a dance, and it was damn nice to watch her flow with me. We seemed a natural team, and I knew I was in trouble.

Chapter Thirty-two

For several weeks, as War Daddy and I became stronger, Ayda and I practiced the movements of fencing.

One thing for certain, Ayda learned fast. Once she became adept at the basic movements, we sparred with wooden poles. I had since collected a second sword from a trader, and during our third week of training together, I presented it to her. She looked at me with a bemused smirk.

"So now we kill each other?" she asked.

"That's not really the plan." I chuckled. "But it is time to mix in real swords so that you become comfortable with their actual weight."

We didn't begin by sparring with each other; that would have been much too dangerous. Instead, we practiced the basic movements over and over again. The weight of the sword changed how one moved and, therefore, it was almost like beginning all over again. Even I, having not used an actual sword during my tournaments, but rather a fencing foil, found the old-world rapier heavier than my liking.

"This isn't nearly as easy as it looks in the movies," she commented after one particularly difficult workout.

"Nothing is," I said, noting the particular way her robe hugged her body on this surprisingly cool morning.

"Do you see," she said, standing next to me and pointing at War Daddy, who was at present playing fetch with a village boy.

I nodded. War Daddy appeared to have most of his strength back, and his wounds had healed marvelously. I had removed the stitches a week ago and saw no sign of infection. For the past few days, just as he had in my mountain cabin, I caught him sitting by Mahdi's front door or pacing before the open windows. He could have left, certainly. But I knew he was waiting for me. Despite being content here, I couldn't help but think about some little girl out there not knowing what had happened to her guide dog.

"Perhaps it's time we get moving again?" I said to Ayda, feeling the sadness and regret well up in me, for I did not want to leave this place of paradise, with its sparkling twin pools, gentle old men, and lively festivities. After all, the village musical prodigy had given me a few pointers, and I had made great gains with the instrument, so much so that I often joined a group of those beating drums and strumming guitars. Most important, I had grown closer to Ayda. So much so, that I had begun thinking about her as something more than a friend.

"Normally, I would agree, but the sunrise this morning tells me we better stay put for a couple of days."

"What?" I wrinkled my brow and turned to face her. "What does the sunrise have to do with how and when we travel?"

"Unless I miss my guess," she began, "I think we will be hit by a pretty ugly sandstorm by late afternoon to evening."

"How do you know this?" I asked.

She smiled sadly. "When you grow up in the desert, you learn to look for the signs—everyone does. A sandstorm like the one that is coming could completely wipe out an entire caravan... or even a tribe. Let's pray the storm doesn't close us in."

"Close us in?"

"By the direction that it is taking, it is possible it will drift enough sand across the oasis for it to block our exit." She pointed to the sheer rock cliffs serving as the primary exit.

"You know the direction it is taking?" I asked, unable to hide the skepticism in my voice.

"Call it an educated guess."

"And you know all of this by looking at the sunrise?"

"It is a very telling sunrise," she said, and smiled. "Now, I must warn the others. We are going to have an interesting next few days."

***

Surprisingly enough—for me, anyway—Ayda was right on the money with her prediction. By late afternoon, a sandstorm, the likes of which I couldn't have imagined in my wildest dreams, blasted in from the northeast.

I also wasn't expecting the temperature to plunge to damn near freezing. I prayed the tent we had barricaded Jake and Chester behind held up. Meanwhile, Mahdi's simple dwelling seemed to sway under the onslaught, all while I was certain we were being buried alive. I mean, I could hear the stuff piling up just outside the walls. Mahdi and I had boarded the windows, and had done so for the elderly around town. Granted, at the time. I had thought it a fool's errand.

Now, the boarded windows shuddered, and sand seeped through any opening it could find. Sprinkles of the stuff pelted me from even within the home.

When Mahdi retired to his bedroom, Ayda came to me with a heavy blanket. "We are probably going to need this."

"We?" I asked, noting she'd brought only the one covering.

She smiled shyly and surprised me to no end when she wrapped the two of us together with the blanket. And thus began the end of our platonic relationship. Of course, I couldn't accuse her of arranging the sandstorm, but I couldn't help but think the way in which we spent that night under that blanket had been arranged, somehow. Regardless of how it happened, she certainly removed any doubts I might have had concerning how she felt about the chemistry between us when, due to our proximity, she invited me into a long, deep and passionate kiss. From that point forward, there simply wasn't any way to stop a very different kind of storm that had been building inside the both of us.

I'd broken away from that first passionate kiss to send a glance in the direction of War Daddy. I wasn't sure if I was asking for his approval or not, but for some odd reason I needed it. He panted, drooled, and raised his black gums in what I could only surmise was a smile. At least, I'd like to think it was.

And the dog appeared to be giving off an 'about damn time' vibe.

Chapter Thirty-three

A few days after the sandstorm subsided, myself, Ayda, and many of those who lived permanently within the oasis, shoveled a great deal of the sand that had mostly covered the path out. Remarkably, War Daddy dug, too.

Now, with the dog back to full strength, and the path clear before us, there was no further reason I could delay the inevitable. For the second time in my life, I was going to leave the oasis, but this time, I found it a lot harder to do.

During a lunch of soup and bread, Ayda sensed a change in my mood.

"You are sad," she said.

I was. We had been in the oasis for two months, at first while I healed, and then later while War Daddy's own significant wounds healed. Now, I could find no further excuse to stay. The problem was... living here in this simple hut with Ayda in the next room and War Daddy ever present felt a lot like a real home.

I merely nodded at her statement.

She came over to me and sat on my lap, wearing her full robe. She put her arms around my neck and rested her head on my shoulder. "You need only to ask, doctor."

I didn't say anything right away; indeed, I was not entirely sure what she had met. But I took a chance and said, "Would you like to come with us, Ayda?"

"To travel halfway across the desert, to destinations unknown, with a bumbling foreigner and his oversized, shaggy dog?"

"Er, yes."

"I would love to, Doctor Shaye."

***

Saying goodbye a second time was, perhaps, hardest of all.

Mahdi hugged us warmly and saw us to the edge of the oasis. With the camels fully stocked, Ayda and I set out through the canyon walls, overflowing with fresh piles of sand, looking a good deal different than from my first pass through here, back when I had been alone with War Daddy and the camels.

Now, of course, I had a very special someone with me, someone who sat high upon Chester, solely a pack animal no more; indeed, he carried the most precious cargo of all.

With Ayda's instruction, I would learn that nomads tend to move from one oasis to another, and, depending upon many factors, stay a certain length of time at each. Additionally, the desert offered only so many water holes, and some of them were only seasonal.

We talked books and I was shocked at the extent to which she had read the great classics of world literature. Though she had started reading much later in life, she had gone into it with an enormous amount of hunger for the great depth of meaning within. Dickens, Hemingway, Hawthorne, Crane, Irving, Dumas, Steinbeck, even Chekov and Dostoyevsky were among the great works that occupied dozens of miles of our conversation over the desert sand.

Later, as we talked about art and politics, we discovered that our lives and our philosophies of living, though formed in different worlds and by different factors, were incredibly similar. I honestly couldn't remember discussing anything in such depth with anyone; that is, before that long trek across the sand.

Our conversations continued as we passed under blazing skies and glittering stars, as smaller sand-storms came and went, as days turned to weeks.

At night, we would lie together, exploring each others' bodies, but always resisting the ultimate temptation. She was, after all, a virgin, and I a foreign man. For me to lie with her, I knew I would need to marry her. And so I would not tarnish her or her body. But I could not stop my lips or my hands, from exploring every inch of her.

More than anything, I couldn't remember having been so happy in a long time.

No, not quite. Make that ever.

***

"That is my father's caravan," she said after we'd topped a sand dune on a particularly scorching day. How the camels and War Daddy doggedly continued through the hot sand, day after day, I didn't know, but my respect for all three creatures had long since reached ridiculous heights.

I looked to where she pointed and could only see a rising cloud of dust in the distance. "How do you know that it's not a caravan of raiders or thieves or black market traders?" I asked. It had been a few months since the two of us had been in captivity of such a bad sort. I, for one, wasn't all that eager to be going back.

"The formation. The pace. The size. The location." She shrugged. "I just know."

I considered challenging her on that point, but I had already learned my lesson with the sandstorm and decided to just take her word for it. Besides, the eagerness gleamed in her eyes. I knew she longed to be with her father. No one could be that eager, and be wrong. Or so I hoped.

We caught up with the caravan that evening.

They had begun to settle in for the night, with many tents already appearing. The moment someone recognized Ayda, a long, loud chorus of cries and chants erupted throughout the tribe. Those chants and the news of her return apparently reached her father, for soon he was riding hard along the dusty line of tents, on a camel of his own.

"My daughter!" he cried out in Triundic.

In a phenomenal display of, um, camelmanship, or whatever it was called in these parts, he deftly swung off his particularly large mount and sank to his knees. He pressed his head three times into the sand before he allowed either of us to dismount. To my great surprise, he promptly ignored his daughter and took me into a large, plush tent still in the process of being erected. He seated me in what I now knew to be the place of honor. Water and all of the best foods were brought to me. I couldn't help but notice that Ayda had been left outside.

After a few more bewildering minutes of this, I finally asked in English, knowing his daughter had taught him the language. "Are you not glad to see your daughter? Why is she not with us?"

"There will be much time to sit with my daughter, kiss her, embrace her and hear her stories, but for the moment, the greatest honor that I can show her is to honor the man who has brought her back to me," he responded with a broad grin. He introduced himself as Hakim. "I have heard your tale of bravery, my friend."

"My tale?"

"Surely news of your escape with my daughter, along with that dog of yours, would have reached us by now. We see and speak to many such passing parties."

"Okay, yeah. That makes sense. But it isn't quite like you think. The real hero is the dog."

"War Daddy? This is your dog, no?" he asked.

"Er, yes."

"Ah, he is a magnificent creature. I've heard of his exploits too. Yes, truly an honor, the both of you, man and beast. Now, you are quite comfortable and might rest easy, then?"

"I lack only War Daddy," I responded. "He does not leave my side."

I could tell my request struck him as unusual by the expression that crossed his face. It must have been highly irregular for them to invite any animal into their tents, let alone a dog.

He pondered a moment, then finally nodded. "Please forgive my oversight." He exited the tent and returned at once with War Daddy. The furry slobber machine had, apparently, been waiting right outside the flap.

As I reclined on the soft cushions and felt myself beginning to relax, I wondered if Hakim had finally gotten around to greeting his daughter—or if their people might have other customs and rituals taking place in preparation for receiving her. Either way, I'd eaten a full meal and drank plenty of water. War Daddy, I noted before I slipped off to sleep, had taken a position near the tent flap, keeping watch over me, as always.

***

After a very long and restful nap, I bathed and dressed in fresh garments of fine silk, in the tradition of those in the tribe.

A great feast had been prepared in my honor and to celebrate Ayda's return. Although I could see her across the way and we exchanged glances often, I still had not had the opportunity to come into contact with her since our arrival. Well-wishers surrounded both of us, as well as tribesmen bearing all sorts of gifts.

Once everyone had finished eating, Ayda came toward me with a broad smile on her face. Finally, we had a moment to sit together.

"You have made quite an impression on everyone," said Ayda.

"I am overwhelmed with their attention."

"You are humble."

"I merely put a bullet in a lock," I said earnestly. "I do not deserve such honor."

"And Ahmed put a bullet in your head." She poked me in the forehead. "Well, tried to. You helped, Doctor Shaye. You may think it something small to do, but if you had not 'put the bullet in the lock' I do not want to even think where I might be now. Because of you, I am here with my family... and with you."

"And War Daddy," I said.

She laughed. "And him, of course."

It was good to hear her laughter again. I'd heard it a great deal throughout the days we traveled the desert, but even this short time since we'd been back with her people felt much too long.

Out of nowhere, a great mob of children surrounded us, perhaps every kid in the tribe. They dragged, pushed and crowded us into a cleared area where everyone had been dancing for hours. Not certain of what I was doing, I simply did the best that I could with what little grace I possessed. I couldn't tell if the tribe delighted in my feeble effort to dance or if I genuinely entertained them, but I saw nothing but smiles among them as they looked on.

Amazingly, remarkably, I think I fit right in.

My two left feet and all.

Chapter Thirty-four

It would take two more days for the tribe (and one foreigner and his dog) to move through the world of drifting sand and rolling dunes before we came to another oasis.

During that time, I saw little of Ayda and had become essentially another member of the tribe. They all expected me to pull my weight. The tent of luxury set up to honor me was no longer provided and I had to make do with my own things. None of that bothered me as much as Ayda's conspicuous absence—and I wasn't dealing with it well. All of that changed when we arrived at Al Bishah.

To say that Al Bishah hadn't been built up and commercialized like Oroug Bani seemed to be a rather silly way of putting it, because neither of them had much of what Westerners would call "services." However, Al Bishah, a great deal more primitive, barely qualified as more than a glorified waterhole in the desert. I could only liken it to Kramer Junction on the highway between Barstow and Bakersfield—only Kramer Junction at least had a Burger King and a truck stop. Okay, so they were nothing alike, really, although they served the same purpose.

In the desert, camels were the cars and semi-trucks, all rolled into one. Just like their vehicular counterparts, camels needed fuel, as did the travelers. The oases scattered throughout the desert provided that fuel in the form of water. Essentially, my perspective had changed dramatically and those oases had become heavenly havens to me. Though the desert still stretched off endlessly to every side, that little patch of water and green helped to restore my soul, as it did everyone's.

"Are you ready to set up shop?" Ayda asked, seemingly coming out of nowhere.

I began to wonder if being able to predict sandstorms and knowing the identity of a caravan by its dust cloud weren't the only magic tricks that she knew how to perform—like disappearing. Maybe that book she wanted really did contain magic? Nah. Now I know I've been in the sun too long.

"Set up shop?" I asked.

"Yes, there are many who would like to have you check their teeth and even look at their wounds," she replied.

"I don't know how long my supplies will last, but I'll do the best I can," I said. By supplies, I meant some suspect cotton balls I had been provided and some rubbing alcohol to disinfect my scalpel, pliers, and mirror all of which had seen better days. I had a dwindling supply of clove oil, which I used as a natural anesthetic for tooth extraction. It dulled some of the pain, but certainly not all of it.

Anyway, I expected her to disappear after that brief exchange, but she just stood there and looked at me. She seemed to be waiting for something. "Yes?"

"I am here to help you," she responded. "Your nurse, as it is."

"Lucky me." I replied.

I'd practiced dentistry for many years and had made a very good living at it. It had provided me with a large house, a number of cars, a decent investment portfolio and a great deal of prestige— that is, up until I started using booze to numb my senses. What I had been doing for the needy in East Sahara, however, rewarded me in a way far beyond all those trappings I had accumulated.

Young, old, rich and poor came, even travelers not part of the tribe, but who'd been staying at the oasis and had heard of me. I worked as quickly as I could, seeing patients from dawn until dusk, well in excess of my usual office hours back in California. Granted, given the available equipment here, I still practiced rather primitive dentistry, but it vastly exceeded anything the people coming to me had ever had access to in their entire lives. My request for more supplies was quickly met. The good thing about traveling with a caravan of traders was that someone, somewhere, had—or could get—what I needed.

Days melted into the next. I fell into bed at night, exhausted, though I kept up that pace for six days. On the seventh day, the number of patients finally dwindled, a lucky break, because my supplies had almost all run out.

Not only was the work rewarding, it allowed me to spend more time with Ayda. We made a great team. She kept everyone coming in an organized fashion and even learned to separate them according to their needs, which helped me do several of the same procedures at once.

"That's the last of them," Ayda announced, coming into the tent about mid-afternoon on the seventh day. In a nearby plastic bag, I had what seemed like several pounds of rotted, putrid and twisted teeth. Since no medical waste disposal services existed out here, they'd go into a burning pit later.

"That's good, because, unless I get to somewhere where I can restock my supplies, we are officially out of business—"

Her lips fell upon mine, hungrily kissing me, her tongue darting and dancing and flicking, a fleshy swordplay that I needed more than I realized.

"For helping my tribe," she said, when she finally pulled back, smiling.

I found myself gasping and unsteady on my feet. She led me to the nearby cushions and eased me down. She kissed me deeply once more, then stood straight. "Sleep, my hero."

As I lay back against the cushions, she opened the tent flap. She slipped away and War Daddy trotted in and lay by my side in a cloud of dust. Automatically, I reached between his ears and scratched his woolly fur. He let out a loud sigh.

"You and me both, buddy," I said as my eyelids grew heavy and I drifted off to sleep.

Chapter Thirty-five

With our stay in Al Bishah much too short for my liking, I decided the length of time in each oasis probably had a great deal to do with trading for supplies and restocking, rather than just a place to hang out.

Needless to say, I awakened the following morning to find the caravan preparing to pull out. By the time the sun broke over the horizon, we were well on our way into the desert, the oasis growing smaller and smaller behind us.

"I suppose I should be trying to help you get home instead of wandering around with a band of nomads," I said to War Daddy. "You have been very patient."

For now, War Daddy seemed content to follow the tribe. Somewhere, that young girl had to be pining for him, alone in a world without sight. Though, I suppose I shouldn't be *too* melodramatic.

The girl obviously has parents since I didn't think orphanages handed out service dogs. My big beautiful dog being content to wander at my side into the desert simultaneously provided a sense of inner peace as it did guilt. For each minute he spent with me, he did not spend with that child who had so lovingly embraced him. And for that matter, I still didn't understand how, exactly, I had seen that—or knew what she looked like, or even that she existed at all. It pained me to think about being separated from him, but that girl needed him far more than I.

Later, as I road side by side with Ayda, she asked if she could resume her sword training.

I smiled. "As you wish."

"Tonight, at camp, I will prepare a place for us to practice." And without waiting for a response, she snapped the reins of her camel and rode on ahead.

"I guess we're training tonight," I said to War Daddy.

"Woof."

***

As the temperature began to cool with the coming of darkness, the caravan halted.

Ayda led me to a place outside of camp that had been prepared for us to continue our training—a small circle lit by torches embedded in the sand, providing more than enough light for us to see. Seemed a waste of fuel, but the daytime was for traveling and was much too hot to practice in. Her father, I learned, had provided the torches.

As we began our warm up, a small crowd of tribal members gathered around the outer edges of the firelight, mostly boys and young men. One such young man, perhaps the oldest of the onlookers, stood with a scowl on his face and crossed arms. I wondered about him. Why out of the entire tribe did he seem the only one displeased with what we did? And if it bothered him so much, why did he stand there watching? I didn't know, but I decided to ignore him.

That night, Ayda and I practiced the basic movements, but it was obvious she had long since mastered them. I could see she was eager for the next level; also, I could see she was eager to impress those watching us, whether she knew it or not. And so, I traded our real swords for the wooden poles, and taught her a number feints and counter-feints. That is, feints within feints... a technique to force your opponent to react, all while a bigger move was planned. I walked her through the move-ments, the arm height, the footwork, the theory behind the move. We worked on feints all night long, while our fire burned low... and the crowd grew in size.

The next evening, after a day of traveling, we resumed where left off. With the crowd of on-lookers growing, I stopped the workout and invited the young boys and girls to join us. They were timid at first, but at Ayda's encouragement, several finally stepped forward. With her help, I arranged them into rows and taught them—with invisible swords—the same basic movements I'd recently taught Ayda. She helped out, too. After that first lesson, she smiled at me in that coquettish way that suggested she thought I might be the cat's meow.

"I am wholly impressed by your ability to teach, Doctor Shaye. You seem like a natural teacher."

I smiled, tickled that I managed to impress her yet again. "All except for Rashid. I don't seem to be reaching him."

"Rashid doesn't approve of me practicing swordplay. Many in the tribe don't. The men, including Rashid, have a more, shall we say, traditional view of the role of women."

"But your father has approved it," I said. "Isn't he traditional?"

"Very," she replied. "But he is also practical. And learning to protect myself from a master fencer is viewed as a good thing. Yet…"

"He has yet to watch our practices, or watch you," I said, sensing where she was going with this.

She took in some air. "His approval only goes so far."

***

Throughout the next several weeks, my group of students not only increased in numbers, but rapidly advanced in skill as well.

Word of my success with the training of the

youth spread, and now others of the tribe watched as well. According to Ayda, I not only pulled my weight in the caravan, but was gaining a great deal of prestige and favor with the elders. Several nights later one of the scouts, who rode on the outer edge of the caravan and kept an eye out for bands of thieves, reported that such a band was in the vicinity and shadowing us. It seemed my prestige would be put to the test.

What I understood of the defensive tactics of the caravan amounted to men dividing into clusters, each of which had to maintain its position and defend against any attackers. Having played some football in high school, it reminded me of a zone coverage. I knew, essentially, if every member tended to their particular zone, that the zone would not be beaten. Of course, this was life and death. Not a Hail Mary from Tom Brady.

To my great surprise, Hakim sent his daughter to stay in my tent for protection, personally dropping her off with a curt nod, before rushing off to tend to the fortifications of the caravan. I noted she had brought her sword. I also noted she had brought two pistols. One for me and one for her. Both had full magazines. I planned to guard her with my life. Her and War Daddy.

With the tribe on high alert, the bastards waited until just before first light before attacking. The shrill scream of someone who had undoubtedly met the wrong end of a scimitar threw the camp into chaos.

I told Ayda to stay with War Daddy, and she did... just long enough for me to slip out of my tent. It dismayed me beyond reason to find her next to me, sword and pistol drawn. War Daddy was by her side. Grr.

I had never thought I would ever need to shed the blood of another man with a sword, nor had I imagined Ayda would be called upon to do so either when I started training her. I had begun the exercises and the movements as a way to regain my strength and vitality, but teaching her had been a way of passing our lonely hours together.

Unfortunately, I didn't have any time to try talking her back into the tent. Men rushed out of the shadows, straight at us. I fired my pistol, as did Ayda, and we circled, back to back, as thieves pitched to the sand or took cover. We did, too.

More attackers appeared, and were met by the firing of many pistols by us and others in our group. Truth be known, I feared that I might be hit by friendly fire. Although dressed as a traditional nomad, I had no knowledge of the skill or fortitude of those fighting with me. Then again, I had no knowledge of my own skill or fortitude. I'd hardly faced down thieves before. The alley didn't quite count, as War Daddy had done most of the fighting.

Now, even in the throes an attack, I was pleased by my calm resolve. Where it came from, I don't know. I had competed at high levels in college, and fought nerves. Here, there were no nerves. Just reaction. And I reacted by taking aim at another human being, even now, and pulling the trigger. The man grabbed at his heart and pitched forward over a crate. I had, I was certain, just killed a man. Meanwhile, next to me, Ayda fired her own pistol until it was out of bullets. Ours emptied at about the same time.

We raised our swords.

Some of the thieves, also out of ammo, attacked us with long knives and scimitars. I stepped in front of Ayda, and she promptly stepped around me and met the first of the attackers head on. Okay, wow. Around us, some weapons still fired, but the *pop-pop-pop* of gunfire waned as bullets were spent and dead fingers grew cold.

Swift and fierce, Ayda met his curved scimitar with confidence to spare. I quickly cut off the charge of my own attacker, slicing my blade across his sword arm, damage enough to get him to cry out and drop his weapon and flee. I didn't have it in me to plunge my weapon into the man, to use my skill to kill a lesser opponent, even if he did have murder in his own eyes. Shooting a man in the dark is a far cry different than facing him from across a blade. I merely wanted him done with so that I could keep an eye on Ayda.

Apparently, she had no such qualms about ending a human life with her weapon, for when I turned to her, I caught her parring a big, arching hack from her opponent, slip to the side, and sink her blade deep into the man's throat. He pitched to his side and reached for his throat, but he was dead before I could reach him. Meanwhile, War Daddy had another man pinned to his back. I couldn't bear the sight of seeing another man's throat ripped out and so I called the dog over and commanded the man to run, which he did, scrambling to his feet and dashing off into the night. You're welcome. That done, I had no more takers, and neither did Ayda.

As the remaining scoundrels fled for the hills, a loud wail erupted from the center of the camp. "Mother!" said Ayda, and rushed to the wailing woman. I only barely kept pace with her sprinting form. I couldn't help but note the half dozen bodies that littered the camp... and not all of them the thieves. We had lost some good men.

Soon, we came upon the kneeling form of her mother who held the bloody head of her husband, Hakim, in her arms. The tribal leader had very clearly suffered a fatal wound to the side of his head. A gunshot. More wails joined her—and not just for the fallen tribal leader. Many had lost loved ones tonight. I watched Ayda comfort her mother, who continued holding Hakim's head in her lap as she rocked back and forth in her grief. Tears streamed down the cheeks of the woman I had come to admire greatly... if not outright love.

I had once heard a Bible verse in Sunday School as a child and it came to mind that very moment. "Grief was swallowed up in victory." What I witnessed was the complete opposite. Though we had slaughtered dozens of attackers and sent the others fleeing for their lives, the loss of Hakim and other tribesmen far outweighed any elation that ought to have come from our victory.

***

I wish that I could say that my skills as a "healer" were of use that night, but sadly, there was only so much I could do for gunshot wounds and many deep sword lacerations.

I did the best I could for the wounded, using up the remainder of my antibiotics and sewing supplies. I was, by far, a better dentist than doctor. For the people of Ayda's tribe, however, I was all they had, and by my estimate I had probably saved three or four this morning who might have otherwise died.

All told, we lost six men, including Hakim. The bandits had lost eighteen. Easily the worst morning of my life.

The funeral had been a somber affair, with the bodies wrapped in shawls anointed with spices and oils, and buried deep beneath the sands. According to Ayda, the bodies would be exposed in weeks or months, undoubtedly to be devoured by vultures and roaming jackals. She said this matter-of-factly, without emotion. The anointed shawls would keep some of the animals at bay, but others would tear through them, eventually. She seemed to accept this and so did I.

After the burial ritual, in which many of the elders spoke highly of the fallen, I eventually found myself alone with Ayda. It had been a hard few days. I'd been busy performing emergency surgeries, while she saw to her father's funeral. Now, the strain on her showed clearly. I saw something else, too, something I hadn't seen, even when she had been abducted on the streets of Urwadi: hopelessness.

I pulled her into me and she broke down. In-between sobs, she said, "I feel so lost, Shaye. So alone and empty, and I just don't know what to do with myself. I can't live without my father."

Later, alone in my tent with War Daddy, a young man informed me that I had been summoned to meet with the elders.

I wasn't sure what interest the elders might have in me; after all, I'd been thanked profusely for the roles that I'd played in helping to protect the tribe and tending to the wounded.

The six elders sat in a semi-circle. As I approached, I bowed deeply. They nodded deeply in return. Ayda, I noted, stood directly behind them, but stepped between them and stood by my side, acting as my interpreter. She squeezed my hand and released it.

"First," said Mumbadi, the senior member of the tribe, as translated by Ayda, "the elders recognize the enormous contribution that you and your training of our young men—and women—made to the defense of the tribe. There is no doubt in anyone's mind that, due to the strength of the attackers, had you not been among us and shared your skill, we might have been overrun."

"I am happy to have been of service," I said, bowing again. "The tribe has become, in many ways, my home, too."

Ayda translated quickly. Mumbadi continued: "I am pleased to hear that, Dr. Shaye, because we have a special favor to ask of you."

"I will do all that I can to honor your favor."

Next to him, one of the other elders handed him a short, heavily jeweled scimitar. I'd seen the sword before, and I was pretty certain it belonged to the late leader, Hakim. Next to me, Ayda stared at it with shimmering eyes.

Mumbadi stood and came over to me, speaking as Ayda translated: "With the passing of Hakim, we have also lost our leader. Although an unlikely choice, your name came up as a possible interim leader. Your devotion to the dog, to Ayda, to the tribe's welfare has not gone unnoticed. Your healing hands, your skill with the blade, and your bravery on the battlefield are more than impressive. The interim role is ceremonial in nature, although some decisions would need to be made here and there. The tribe, of course, will eventually elect a long-term leader, but we need one now, to guide us, for it is our way."

Ayda paused, knowing where this was going. I think my jaw had long since dropped open.

Mumbadi continued, "Doctor Shaye, would you do us the honor of accepting this sword, which has been the symbol of leadership for our tribe since time immemorial? By doing so, you will agree to guide our tribe, even if only temporarily, with all your heart and soul and wisdom?"

I looked at Ayda and, amazingly, her shocked expression had turned into what could only be described as hope. To my astonishment, she nodded slowly, giving me her approval.

Perhaps most astonishing of all were the words that next escaped my mouth. "Yes. I accept this great honor."

Chapter Thirty-six

And so it was.

There had been little ceremony. The tribal council edict was law, and they had proclaimed me the interim leader until they found another. The tribe had accepted their choice. Or, rather, most of the tribe had. I caught glares from Rashid, but that was nothing new.

The assumption from that point forward was that, because of my limited language abilities, I would need Ayda by my side. Not just to translate, but to show me the ways of the tribe; in particular, the ways of a leader. Who better than the daughter of the former leader? The tribe, I would learn, was a world in and of itself, and I had much to learn.

A week after accepting the responsibility of leading the tribe, I found myself with Ayda at the top of a dune, looking out across the vast sea of sand toward the setting sun and feeling both lost and found.

She pointed toward the horizon and asked what I saw. Although I had been lost in my thoughts and wondering how War Daddy fared; after all, we had taken quite a detour from returning the big fellow home. Thus far, he had trotted by my side, without being restless to get back to the girl.

I said, "I see a streak of red shooting up through an area of violet. Very unusual."

She said nothing, and waited. Hot wind blew, pulling at her loose robes, and slapped at my jeans still stained with blood. War Daddy stood next to me, contemplating eternity.

It finally dawned on me. "A sandstorm is coming."

"Very good, Doctor Shaye."

"From which direction and when?"

"The red streak, you'll note, appears in the northwest. Tell me, how far up into the sky does the red light reach?"

"In miles?" I asked.

"Think percentages," she said.

"The streak occupies maybe a third of the sky, maybe more."

"I would agree, and from that information, we can make our prediction. We have, roughly, thirty hours before the storm arrives."

"So where do we need to go and how soon do we leave?"

"There is a wadi to the west," she said. I could tell by the look in her eyes that she was proud of the fact that I was already thinking ahead. A wadi, I knew, was a deep ravine that should shield us from the brunt of the sandstorm.

"How long will it take us to get there?"

"About ten hours of travel time." She studied my face as I made my calculations.

Although the tribe sometimes traveled by night, Hakim often chose not to. As nomads, they traveled if and when they needed to. As it was, we didn't need to break camp. It had been a tough week, and I wanted the tribe to rest. By my estimates, we had ten hours to spare.

"We'll leave at dawn," I said.

"And what if another caravan gets there first? It is a well-known location, desirable for many nomadic tribes to shelter the many sandstorms."

"We share politely?" I suggested.

"There is room enough for only one caravan, doctor."

"What are you suggesting?"

"You know what I'm suggesting, Shaye."

I did, and the answer was obvious. "It's a race, then."

"Indeed."

"Then we need to get moving. We can rest in the wadi."

"Spoken like a true leader. I'll inform the others."

***

Within the hour, the camp had been broken down.

With Ayda riding beside me in the lead, she showed me how to follow the stars; in particular, which formation led where and at what time of the year. I tried to remember everything she said, but mostly, I enjoyed being with her in the open air under the living sky. As always, War Daddy trotted by my side.

Although some grumbling came from the tribe, I kept a fast pace. As dawn broke, we reached the high stone walls of the wadi. There had been some anxious moments as we drew near to it just as a dust cloud came into view on the horizon nearby. We quickened our pace, arriving in the wadi just before the other caravan.

"Perhaps there's room for them," I said, eyeballing the canyon and wondering if there would be even enough space for just our tribe.

"Relax, doctor," said Ayda. "There is another wadi six hours from here. If they do not delay, they will be fine." She pointed. "Look, they have already veered toward it. It might be a close call for them, but they should make it in time."

The tribe did not waste a single movement setting up camp and securing the animals. Coming out of a sandstorm only to find your camels miles away—or dead—was not something that a good leader would allow to happen.

The sandstorm hit with a roaring vengeance. To me, it sounded like a runaway freight train. Hundreds of them. Thankfully, Ayda had begun to share my tent with me. Everyone understood that her father, prior to his death, had sought me out to protect her, and my protection would continue indefinitely. It provided a good reason for her to lay by my side each night.

As the storm raged outside, beyond the sheltering confines of the high-walled wadi, Ayda and I found ourselves lost in a storm of our own making. Her smooth, dark skin against my pale skin made as artful a contrast as the setting sun upon the darkening sky. During that storm, I was certain our love had grown to an altogether new level.

Chapter Thirty-seven

Two days later, we reached Melmud under my "leadership."

In reality, we wouldn't have made it through the sandstorm if it hadn't been for Ayda telling me what to do, as well as the entire tribe knowing a sandstorm was coming and the best place to take shelter from it well before I did. I didn't try to fool myself into thinking the tribe was successful because of my leadership. I knew better.

The one person truly suited to leading the tribe was, in my opinion, Ayda. The tribe hadn't appointed her the new leader for only one reason—she was a woman. The elders had split on accepting her on that factor alone. My discomfort concerning my inflated role and position in the tribe became even more evident to me as we settled in at Melmud and those who met and traded with us gave me a great deal of honor. Ayda had been groomed by her father from an early age to lead. Perhaps he had hoped that someday the tribe would accept a woman. But, for now, I was that leader, deserving or not.

I remained under constant scrutiny while moving about Melmud by everyone around me. Amazingly, my reputation preceded me. I'd become known as a healer and a warrior. A rare combination in these parts, apparently. In fact, because of my presence in Melmud, people who wanted to have me care for them overwhelmed our tribe. Because of the crowds wanting to see me, it put not only Ayda and me, but the entire council of elders, into an awkward dilemma. Attempting to trade and obtain what we needed as well as run an emergency dental office, became an enormous burden on everyone. Most of all, I felt extremely guilty about War Daddy and keeping him from that little girl who needed this dog back by her side.

Three nights later, while staring out the tent flap at the pacing dog, I knew my time with the tribe had come to an end. At least, for this stretch. After much soul searching, I decided that I needed to see my mission through to the end. I needed to return War Daddy home.

With a heavy heart, I summoned the council members, including Ayda.

***

Though Ayda initially struggled against the idea, even she understood that I did the right thing.

However, she had not expected me to put forth a motion for her to be my replacement.

"I'm not translating that," she said, shaking her head.

"You must tell them."

"But it isn't my place to suggest your replacement."

"Ayda, you're not suggesting my replacement. I'm doing the suggesting and you're doing the translating."

"Still..." she replied.

The elders watched our exchange with mild perplexity on their weathered faces.

"I will tell them myself if you refuse," I said through a fake smile and gritted teeth.

She nearly said something snarky—we both knew just how poor my language skills were—but finally relented. I listened hard, making sure my intentions were expressed. From what I gathered she had shared my request. Her words were met with silence. Finally, Mumbadi nodded and asked us to give the council a chance to consider my request. We would be summoned shortly.

The moment we stepped away from the circle of elders, Ayda turned on me. "You could have warned me you, you know."

"Then you would have fought me tooth and nail. And I've seen your nails."

"But why would you suggest that I lead the Saba-al-Bawadi?" This was, of course, the name of her tribe.

"Because you are *already* their leader," I replied. At present, our camp sat on the outskirts of town, as common for desert nomads who typically shunned city life. Above, the blue sky was clear and eternal.

"No, Shaye, you hold that position."

"Only temporarily. It is you who are guiding your people."

"They've become your people, too. Have you not fought for them? Killed for them?"

"Yes and no. They have been kind enough to take me in and accept me as one of them, and have honored me far beyond what I deserve, but I am an interloper. I am not only unfamiliar with the language and customs, but I am also not the person who ought to be leading these people. Ayda, you are best suited for that job."

"But they will never accept a woman as their leader."

"Some won't. But the others will recognize your wisdom, your skills, and your leadership. Over time, as the tribe remains secure and prospers, as I know they will under your leadership, most if not all will come around. Once War Daddy is home, I will return."

She opened her mouth to say something, but a messenger ran up to us, bringing word that the council had requested our presence.

"The recommendation of the chosen interim leader of the tribe has been taken with a significant amount of consideration and discussion," said

Mumbadi. "The arguments made concerning Ayda's qualifications is a solid one. The arguments against her are weak and baseless. It is obvious to all that she possesses all of the skills necessary to be a great leader.

"Alas, we are not ready to rule one way or the other. Since the Saba-al-Bawadi have never been led by a woman, we feel the entire tribe should have a say in this, not just the elders. Our question will be put before the tribe this evening. If anyone objects, then there will be a challenge between the one who objects and Ayda, daughter of Hakim. The winner will lead the tribe and the other will be banished from it. The terms are harsh, but with such terms, it will prevent frivolous claims."

And with that, we waited for nightfall.

Chapter Thirty-eight

Of course, Rashid objected.

As much confidence as I had in Ayda's leadership skills, as well as how I had seen her advance rapidly in her sword training with me, watching her fight Rashid was not going to be easy. Although the match would take place using wooden sparring swords rather than real blades, I remained concerned for her safety, unsure that she could beat the power-hungry young tribesman. Truth be known, I had expected his challenge the moment Mumbadi announced the council's recommendation, and was not disappointed.

Now, as they prepared to square off within the ring of torchlight, the entire tribe assembled in the shadows, speaking in subdued tones. As he stretched and practiced with his own wooden weapon, I noted once again that Rashid was a large young man by East Saharan standards. I had no doubt that he was a vicious fighter, too, based on his temperament. He'd made it clear that he did not approve of a woman in the role of leadership; in fact, he hadn't approved of her being trained by me in the first place.

The match would be decided by two out of three falls. The council had selected a judge known for his impartiality and skill in hand-to-hand combat. I knew the man, a good man. I trusted him.

I stood with the council members, worried sick. A pole to the side of the head could cause serious harm, as would a pole driven into the abdomen. The woman I had come to love had been put into danger... by me, no less, and my need to return War Daddy home. Of course, I did not have to recommend her for the role of leader. Then again, Ayda did not have to go along with the idea either.

Except she had, because she wanted this. I knew it, and the whole tribe knew it.

As the torches flickered and the crowd grew restless, the judge raised a hand, looked at both fighters, who both nodded, and lowered his hand sharply. The match began with both contenders circling each other. Never had I felt more sick. Well, seeing War Daddy in the dog fighting ring was right up there too. This... was different. That woman facing that huge young man was a woman I had grown to love. And this was no sparring match. This was a fight.

I wanted to vomit.

As the two of them continued circling, I

couldn't help but recall the conversation we'd had prior to the fight. "You must use Rashid's arrogance against him," I said. "He expects to win easily. He expects to embarrass you. Attack aggressively and land the first blows. With any luck, his temper will overtake him and that will be his downfall."

My words had no more than repeated themselves in my mind than Ayda pressed her first attack. Her speed and ease of movement was exhilarating to watch. The scowling Rashid was no slouch. He'd been in combat many times, even for his young age. He was a confident and skilled swordsman, and he parried her initial strikes.

Minutes later, after an exchange of strikes, Ayda appeared to make a purposeful misstep and received a blow across the chest that sent her sideways across the sand, giving Rashid the first fall.

"That wasn't exactly the strategy," I told her when we consulted during a brief rest. Like boxers, each had stepped back for a breather.

"You said that you wanted to use his arrogance against him," she countered.

"Well, yeah, but I sort of thought that you winning the first fall would have accomplished that purpose."

"I am toying with him. Like they say in America… there's more than one way to skin a cow."

"Cat," I said.

"Who would skin a cat?"

She frowned, and headed into the makeshift ring. I noted she appeared to be timid and scared, and suspected it was all a ruse. It must have worked. Instead of a scowl upon Rashid's face, he sported a wicked grin. Maybe her way of 'skinning a cow' was right in this instance.

Ayda made an opening move that presented a weakness; Rashid rushed in to take full advantage of what I'm sure he believed would lead to her second fall. Instead, she whirled into a risky counter-move that swept his feet out from under him. As he tumbled into the sand, she brought her sword down upon the back of his neck before he could recover, winning her first fall.

"I didn't teach you that one," I said when she came over to me minutes later.

"Rashid taught it to me," she smiled.

"When did he teach you that?" I asked. I'd never seen her train with him and I doubted that she ever had.

"A few minutes ago, during his first attack."

I nodded. Indeed, he had attempted such a move and failed. My God she was a quick learner. When they called her back into the ring and the fight resumed, I realized something else. Ayda actually enjoyed this; indeed, she almost appeared to be toying with Rashid.

Furious over his first fall, he had exploded on her, and delivered a wicked shot to her ribs. But Ayda didn't go down, and that blow couldn't have felt very good; indeed, she sucked air as they circled again. Rashid pressed swinging wildly, too wildly. Ayda ducked under it, and rammed the point of her

pole hard to his mid-section. The bigger man stopped cold, gasped. Ayda stepped away and swung
her pole like a baseball bat, striking the young
man's temple. He lurched to the side and lay
unmoving.

The good news was, the poles were not as thick
and sturdy as bats. These practice rods had wobble
to them and were half as thick as a bat handle. Still,
they had some heft to them, and I was not surprised
to see Rashid only barely begin to regain
consciousness.

Like boxers, he was counted out and the fight
was over.

Ayda, to the cheers of nearly everyone, had
won.

I might have cheered loudest of all.

Chapter Thirty-nine

Images of Ayda's dark body glowing with a mist of sweat, her eyes, deep as the midnight sky, looking down as she rocked back and forth upon me, would haunt me forever. After all, we had made love during our last night together, and I had no doubt in my mind she was a descendant of Queen Sheba herself.

Our final night together had been a mixture of regret and a promise that I would return as soon as I fulfilled a promise I had made. She hadn't quite said she believed what I'd seen in my vision—the blind girl—but she also didn't call me crazy.

The following morning proved bittersweet for me. Saying my goodbyes had been difficult for everyone, though they understood my personal journey, whether or not they agreed with it. I'd barely mounted Jake when War Daddy took the lead and trotted out of camp. I chuckled and shook my head, marveling at the dog's unusual knowing and singular purpose. I heeled the camel and glanced back, hoping to see Ayda one more time, but she was no longer standing where I'd left her. And so it goes.

Now, from my vantage point atop the dune, I watched the caravan wind snake-like over sand and dune. To think that I had once led such a caravan, even for just a short while, blew my mind. Though, I don't really think I 'led' much of anything. Ayda had been the true leader the whole time. However, I did take some personal satisfaction for pushing the tribe past their sexism. With any luck, I would someday have all the time in the world to appreciate my dear Ayda. For now, I had a blind little girl to worry about. A child who didn't even know I existed, and for all I knew could be anywhere in this godforsaken country. I took in some air and looked at War Daddy waiting impatiently next to me.

"Lead the way, fur face."

Not needing to ask him twice, War Daddy turned his nose toward the southeast. As we doubled back on the path the caravan had taken to Melmud, I realized just how far off track I'd taken the ever patient War Daddy.

Ayda's parting words still echoed in my mind: "Trust in fate, Shaye," she had said. "For it will be fate which will bring us back together again."

***

Loneliness and being alone are two different animals.

I'd been alone for many months, but I had never felt lonely. Not with the walking, barking slobber factory always around—and even the two camels offered some companionship.

Now was different, though. For weeks, I had helped and healed and trained those people. I had fought alongside them, buried them, and mourned with them. Most importantly, I had loved one of them deeply, and now I was suffering. I knew a dark cloud of depression hung over me, and I did little to fight it… at least, not at first. But as the days added up, as War Daddy trotted unerringly to the southeast, I felt my spirits pick up. The dog's singular focus couldn't be denied, and it overrode my misgivings and sorrow.

I thought often of Ayda. I visualized her dark eyes looking into mine, the golden tone of her smooth skin and the gentle flowing curves of her body. Her scent still lingered in my nostrils, her touch tingled upon my skin and the sound of her voice continued to haunt me. No, to galvanize me.

Despite the hope that we would be together again someday, it was difficult for me to predict when and how that might happen. Logic said I should simply bring War Daddy to his home and get my ass back to the military base and hop a flight back to the States. Ayda and I came from two totally different worlds, even if she had acclimated to mine more than I felt comfortable in hers. A rational person would leave behind all thoughts of ever being with or seeing Ayda again. That, of course, was much easier said than done.

"Well, buddy," I said, sitting beside a small fire with my fingers tangled in his thick white mane, "are we getting any closer to home?"

For an answer, he looked at me with eyes that seemed to be telling me all sorts of things.

I sighed. "I wish you'd just come right out and tell me where we're going. It would be over with a lot quicker and I could start putting West Sahara behind me and get on with my life."

Not even a bark. In fact, he appeared to shake his head sadly as if to call me a fool.

I sighed and reached for the block flute in my bag. Just as my fingers curled around it, a searing jab of pain burned into my hand.

With a yelp, I yanked it back, and stared in awe at a golden scorpion dangling from it... its stinger deeply embedded in my skin. Before I could even think of what to do, the barb came loose and the critter dropped and scurried off into the night.

Chapter Forty

I'd seen many beautiful sunsets while in the East Saharan desert, but I'd never seen one quite like this.

The sinking sun cast its orange and golden hues upon the sand, seemingly transforming its color into those of the sky. Indeed, sky and sand became one. The dunes rippled in golden waves... or was that the sky? Eventually, the undulating sand seemed to rise up, and took the form of humanoids. The figures flowed toward me, seemingly floating on the surface of the sun.

It seemed I had been visited by the LSD scorpion.

A man who could have been a thousand years old, if a hundred, approached me, radiating light. "You are the healer." His voice had a deep, rich tone that bathed me in comfort. "You have traveled far to be with us."

"I have traveled very far," I said, my throat dry, my tongue fat. Maybe I should have been afraid by their presence, but I wasn't. I figured I was dying, so who cares? Maybe this is what death looked like, at least out in these parts. "Who are you?"

"We are the People of the Sands. I am the Ancient One. You are of the Saba-al-Bawadi," he said, speaking the name of Ayda's tribe.

"Not entirely. I was their leader for a short while, but I really didn't deserve the title. It really belonged to Hakim's daughter. Is your name really the Ancient One?"

He smiled. "You've been stung."

"Yes."

"You are dying."

"I think so, yes."

"Come with me," he said.

I knew I had been too sick to move, but for reasons I couldn't guess at, I found myself standing and following the old man. The sand flowed like a river of golden light. Shimmering trees rose up from its banks. Golden fish leaped from the shallows, only to splash down into the sun-drenched water. We walked beside the river of light for seemingly an eternity before coming to a waterfall. Others stood with us, rising up from the earth itself, each gleaming in radiant beauty. Though it should have shocked me to see people popping out of thin air like that, it felt normal and expected.

To my shock, the others all approached the precipice, and with only a momentary hesitation to admire the view, they leaped. I peered down, watching each figure plummet until they disappeared into an oasis lake, deep blue like a sapphire. It looked beyond beautiful, but *so* far down the drop would surely be fatal. Each man plunged beneath the surface in a glimmering flicker of brilliant light, disappearing... and not to return. Soon, only the old man and myself remained at the cliff's edge. Wait, the water next to me turned to sand, and poured over the edge and filled the basin below, like a massive hourglass.

"Why did they jump?" I asked.

"To show you how easy it is."

"I... I don't want to jump. It is a long way down. And that is sand, I think. Not water."

"We can heal you, Shaye."

"I... I don't know that."

"Of course you don't. We have only just met."

"Then why do you want me to jump off a cliff?"

"The pool beneath you is unlike any pool, Shaye. It is a healing pool."

"Isn't there, you know, another way down? Do I have to jump?"

"What do you think, Shaye?"

I sighed and continued looking down at the impossibly picturesque lake... No, a giant pool of sand. I could see it piling up, higher and higher... I blinked and the water was back, as golden and beautiful as ever. What was happening to me? I was dying, that's what was happening. The water, if anything, felt even farther away. "I think you want me to jump."

"Very good."

"But I am afraid."

"Then you will die in this place."

And with that, the old man jumped from the precipice. I watched his body arch up and out... and descend rapidly down a cliff covered in verdant greenery... only to plunge into the water, far below. I stared at the ripples, waiting for him to surface, but he didn't. The sand seemed to return, burying him.

My God...

Left alone, I had a decision to make. I desired to be whole again. I desired to live and see War Daddy through on this journey. More than anything, I desired to see Ayda again.

But I feared whatever might become of me if I leaped.

Of course, this all had to be a delirious dream, right? Wasn't I, even now, sweating and shaking and dying next to a fire that had long since gone out?

I had to be. Which meant this couldn't be real. The cliff, the old man, the pool of water/sand far below, so distant I could barely see it. I didn't want to die, but I also didn't want to be stranded up here alone. I wanted to live and love and laugh again. I wanted to run with War Daddy, and I *needed* to be with Ayda.

I moved out to the edge of the cliff and closed my eyes. I could do this. What did I have to lose? I was dying anyway...

I tilted... and fell forward. I didn't jump like the old man. No. I merely tilted out, and then I was falling, falling...

Falling...

The wind stung my face as I plunged through the air toward the fiery lake. As I fell, visions of my life passed before me: visions from my youth, from high school, college and dental school. I saw my friends and my family. I relived my wedding, the death of my parents, the pain of my divorce. I saw a bottle of Jack Daniels before me on a table and I reached for it, only to have it explode—just as I felt myself plunge into the lake.

An instant warmth surrounded me, unlike anything I'd felt before. It penetrated my body and filled me completely. All of those things that I had seen as I was falling, those painful memories, disappeared as I sank deeper into the water.

"You are worthy," said a voice. "From this day forward, your heart will know the way home. From this day forward, you will rewrite your story. From this day forward, you will be one of us..."

As I sank within the limitless depths, I saw War Daddy by my side. I saw Ayda—she was even more lovely than my best memories were able to recall her. And I saw Mahdi sitting beside the water in Oroug Bani. Hands appeared before me. They placed a golden scorpion on a golden chain around my neck.

The voice of the Ancient One spoke to me as it

faded away: "An angel watches over you. Yes... an angel..."

***

I found myself lying face-down in the cool sand.

As I came into full awareness of my body, I realized I still lay at the same campsite where the scorpion had stung me. Jake and Chester remained where they should be. My stuff lay undisturbed. Aside from me being several feet off my sleeping mat and face down, I hadn't gone anywhere. At least, not in the physical world.

The memory of the scorpion sting rushed into my thoughts. I had been dying. Or maybe I had died. Was I dead now? The dream. The hallucination. The Ancient Ones. The cliff. Yes, I had surely died. I think.

A cool wind pulled at me. Morning sunlight splashed the horizon. Rapid panting reached my ears. I blinked. A big white, beautiful dog hovered over me, standing guard.

Could I move? Or was this death?

I put weight on my outstretched arm, and rolled over. Amazingly, no pain. No weakness, either. I pushed myself up to a sitting position, and discovered something dangling at my chest, something golden. I ignored it for now.

It wasn't easy to piece together the events that had taken place, but I did my best. After the scorpion sting, I had tried to extract the venom as best I could, but I fell ill anyway. I curled up next to the fire, sweating and shaking. War Daddy had curled up next to me. I reached out and lay a hand on his giant forepaw—and then came the hallucinations. The People of the Sand.

Did I seriously jump off a cliff? No way.

But I had, in my poison-induced coma, or whatever had happened to me. Somehow, some way, I appeared to have come out of it from the other end. And I had slept through the night. I had slept and hallucinated.

Except...

I reached under my shirt and pulled out a gold chain with a golden scorpion attached to it. The scorpion had eyes of sapphires, claws of emeralds and a ruby shard for a stinger. I turned it over in my hands, examining it and trying to figure out how in the hell it had gotten there. This was no hallucination.

I looked at War Daddy. "What happened?"

The big drool factory only stared at me.

"You're sure a lot of help," I said, finding my feet and feeling oddly… refreshed.

Who felt refreshed after a scorpion sting? I didn't know, but I had a long day ahead of me and I was determined to see War Daddy home.

Wherever the heck that might be.

Chapter Forty-one

We emerged from the sand dunes, and soon the path grew rockier. Around us stone hills punched through the desert, themselves bleak and inhospitable. War Daddy seemed to have settled on a well-grooved path that seemed to have been impressed into the rock for centuries, if not eons.

Because of the skills that I picked up while traveling with the Saba-al-Bawdi, I knew I was being followed. Assuming it was Rashid would have been a mistake. A number of desert dwellers might be interested in robbing me, capturing me, and receiving the bounty a black market smuggler in El Alalim offered or—more likely—they just wanted War Daddy.

Watching my back trail, I decided to pull a little trick that I'd read about in a Louis L'Amour novel. I had always loved the American West, gunfighters and that sort of thing. I doubled back using a parallel ravine, settled Jake and Chester at the bottom, and crawled up to the top of a dune where I could get a good look at who followed me.

The trick worked; I spotted Rashid, no friend of mine.

I waited until he disappeared over a rise, and I intersected my former trail and started out across the desert on a path perpendicular to the one we'd been on before. I hoped my little maneuver would separate me from Rashid and he'd continue along the well-beaten path I'd abandoned.

I had no idea where and when I would run into another usable trail that led to anywhere of note, but, for the moment, I contented myself to put distance between us. I would worry about how we would get back on the main trail later. Luckily, War Daddy had a sense like a homing pigeon, and I planned to put it to full use.

My trick seemed to work, because several days later, I still hadn't seen Rashid. We'd settled on a narrow trail that seemed to be a great deal less traveled. I'm not sure this was the road Robert Frost had referred to. I played the block flute at times, talked to War Daddy and the camels at other times, and thought about Ayda all the time...

***

I awoke one morning with a strange feeling.

That inexplicable sensation—somewhere between knowing a significant event would occur and worried that it would—kept me staring up at the brightening sky for a few minutes, trying to make sense of it.

Jake and Chester had an air of blasé laziness to them, so nothing was nearby hunting us. Okay, that was a relief. Maybe this feeling meant I would soon find the reason for my being here. If so, that also meant War Daddy and I would no longer be together. So, yeah. Perhaps my lying there without feeling much need to get up and get moving came from that. In my old life, I'd seen plenty of children doing everything they could to delay walking into the waiting room at my old dental practice.

Right about now, I felt like one of them.

Though, I'd like to think visiting my dental practice hadn't been as emotionally wrenching to kids as the idea of never seeing War Daddy is to me. And speaking of kids… somewhere out there is a little girl who—as much as I hate to admit it to myself—needed him more than I did. It was the entire reason I'd come here.

"What do you think, Fuzz-face?" I asked, turning my head and looking at the pile of white fur lying next to me. "That is why we're here, right? The whole reason for me going to East Sahara is to find this kid…"

He lifted his head and glanced at me with this 'wow, you just don't get it' kind of expression before resting his chin on his paws again. Or at least, that's what I read from it.

"There's more to it than just getting you home?"

War Daddy made the dog version of a 'harrumph.'

"I needed to come to East Sahara for some other reason?"

He again looked at me, almost a 'now you're getting it' gleam in his eyes.

"So you left this kid behind to drag my sorry ass halfway across the earth?"

He groaned.

I mean, amid my drunken depression, I have the occasional memory of trying to ask God, fate, the universe, or whatever for some sign. No, I can't imagine he'd willingly leave behind some innocent kid who can't see to scrape my butt out of the gutter. Maybe it's some kind of cosmic attraction thing. "Fate put us together."

Head tilt, ears perked.

"And you're helping me out because we needed each other." I scratched behind his ears. "Yeah. I can't say coming here was a bad idea. I feel like an entirely different person. Thank you, buddy."

War Daddy crawled a little closer, emitting a frustrated grunt.

"I'm still missing something, aren't I?"

He stared.

Okay. I took that as a yes. But…

"There," said a distant woman's voice.

Startled, I twisted around to peer over my shoulder at… Ayda?

What the hell was she doing standing on a dune out in the middle of nowhere?

War Daddy yawned, then gave me a pointed look… and it hits me. Back in the city he'd taken off into that alley right before those men threw Ayda into the Mercedes. When Ahmed's thugs grabbed us at the camp after that, he hadn't even acted on alert. No way he didn't see them, hear them, or smell them coming—he *let* them grab us. Son of a bitch. That explains the 'you're making me do this the hard way' attitude he gave off.

"You led me to her…"

War Daddy rolled, exposing his belly to me, and panted with a giant tongue-lolling-out grin. I suppose I should be grateful he didn't call me an idiot for taking this long to see it. Or, for that matter, say anything at all, which would have freaked me the hell out.

Then again. He was a dog and maybe I was reading entirely too much into this but... it's almost too much of a coincidence to argue.

I stood and faced the dune behind me to the right. Ayda hurried down the near side, with eight men from the tribe following. Wait... she wasn't a mirage? A figment of my imagination? This was real life?

"No way," I whispered, and found myself rushing across the open sand, expecting her to disappear at any moment. But she didn't. My God, she didn't. She met me a little short of halfway to where I'd camped.

"Shaye…" she gasped.

I nearly swooped her into a hug, but held myself

back due to our having an audience. Instead, we reached for each other's hands, squeezing. My heart insta-swelled at the sight of her, though despite the rush of elation at no longer being apart from this woman who I'd come to love, I couldn't help but worry about her leaving our tribe behind.

Wait... *our* tribe? Well, I suppose it does feel more like home than anywhere else. And at the moment, as I stared into her shimmering eyes, I knew I didn't belong anywhere else.

"Ayda." I pulled her into a brief hug. "What are you doing out here?"

"Coming to find you. What else?" she said with a grin.

"But the tribe needs you more than I do."

"Shaye..." She squeezed and relaxed her grip in my hand. "You are my tribe, too. And much more. I could not sit idle while you roamed the desert searching for some child who might not even exist."

I brushed her hair off her face and smiled. The sight of her filled me with a rush of energy and hope. "She exists, and we will find her. I know it. I am beyond overjoyed to see you, but I can't ask you to put your life, or the lives of your people, at risk for this thing I need to do."

"They came of their own insistence." Ayda stepped back and nodded to them. "Mumbadi claimed he had a vision and I should go to you. He seems to believe War Daddy will lead you to your destiny."

"I believe he already has." In flagrant disregard of the eight men watching us, I leaned in and kissed her.

Her cheeks darkened with a mixture of passion, embarrassment, and playful anger. Together we moved back to my little camp. "This quest you are on will be dangerous. You should not be alone."

"How hard can it be to help him return to this kid?"

"Mrrf," huffed War Daddy, as if to say 'you have no idea.'

"After everything you've been through?" asked Ayda. "I could not allow you to take this risk alone. Besides… I wanted to be with you. Mumbadi and the elders are guiding the tribe in my absence. He did not think I would be away long."

"Well, I suppose we shouldn't keep the old man waiting," I said, aching to kiss her again.

The men, Kasim, Gadi, Farran, Abir, Dawud, Humayd, Mahmoud, and Jamil, approached, smiling and eager to shake hands, reassuring me they all thought of me as a respected member of the tribe.

"Well," I said, glancing over at Jake the camel. "Time to get up."

Both camels regarded me with a stare of indifference, neither making a move to stand.

"Don't suppose you have jumper cables?" I muttered.

"What?" asked Farran.

Ayda laughed.

I held up a hand. "Bad joke. All right. Let's go."

Chapter Forty-two

War Daddy trotted off over the desert with a sense of mission.

I couldn't tell whether his burst of energy came from being proud of me for realizing he had led me to Ayda or relief that the idiot had finally caught on. A part of me still wanted to think of him as an ordinary dog and laugh at myself for attributing anything that happened to the machinations of fate or supernatural circumstance. Of course, I *had* fallen asleep after being stung by a scorpion and woke up wearing an amulet that hadn't been there before.

Unless East Sahara possessed an unusually inept brand of thief who snuck up on people to *give* them things, I had no explanation for where it came from. I also had no explanation for how I so often read more complex thoughts in War Daddy's eyes than any dog should be able to convey. For so long I'd assumed them the product of my mind, what I wanted to hear or what I assumed he would say. But now, as I sat upon my camel turning the scorpion pendant in my fingers, my openness to something… weirder grew.

Ayda rode beside me throughout the day. We followed War Daddy's lead, with the men riding single file behind us. I asked about what had happened with the tribe in the days since my departure, and she filled me in. Much to my relief, little of consequence had occurred beyond the usual migration. Though—and I'm sure she exaggerated—most everyone kept asking her where I'd gone, if I would be okay, if I planned to return. More than what my presence meant for the tribe, it seemed they'd come to feel as if one of their own had gone missing.

War Daddy led us with more focus than usual, trotting into the desert like some sort of white, furry guided missile. I couldn't help but wonder if my realization that fate had put us together so he could lead me to this place, to Ayda, had finally unburdened him of whatever sense of obligation he had to help me. Truth be told, it *did* make me feel guilty that my obtuseness kept him away from that child.

But, in setting out to bring him home… he'd wound up leading *me* home.

I ended up telling Ayda about my vision or dream, and that beautiful lake I jumped into. She listens with noticeable interest but didn't say much, seemingly lost in thought. At least she didn't call me nuts.

We stopped for the night near a cluster of three palm trees around a minuscule lake. It hardly counted as an oasis, and the water was muddy… but water is water out here. The men ran a few jugs of it through a device, basically a series of cloth slings over a pot that filtered the dirt out. Anything to preserve the water in jugs on their camels, and restock the empty ones.

Over a meal of nuts, bread, and dried fruit, the men peppered me with questions about the nature of my journey. I explained my need to return War Daddy to the little blind girl, and how he seemed to finally be making his way back to her. They nodded, knowing full well the mystique surrounding the dog's breed. I also mentioned my concern that Sallah, the man behind my kidnapping, may seek retribution against the Saba-al-Bawdi, purely for my association.

"Nonsense," said Ayda. "Sallah's power is in the cities. His people know nothing of how to sur-vive out here. They wouldn't bother. He would be a fool to send his people against us to avenge the two that War Daddy killed—and killed in self defense, no less."

"Indeed." Mahmoud raised his bowl of food in toast. "He would lose twenty to avenge two, and still fail to do so."

The others nodded and made noises of agree-ment.

A hesitant smile crossed my lips. "So, what you're saying is, I'm safe as long as I roam the deserts with you lot."

Ayda folded her arms, barely resisting the urge to grin back at me and keep a serious expression. "That is precisely what we are saying."

I glanced over at the men, who all sported various degrees of smirks and smiles. "Well, I can certainly think of nowhere else I'd rather be."

Ayda let her smile out and sat close beside me while we finished our meal. Before long, we set up tents for the night, and the two of us finally enjoyed some privacy. Given the close camp and thin cloth walls, neither one of us planned on doing *too* much, but having her in my arms made it difficult to think about anything other than how much I'd missed her... even if it had only been a few days.

We held each other, kissing while our hands explored. Eventually, we reclined on our sides, almost nose to nose. Pretty sure we got into a competition for who could make the other happier for a few minutes.

"Tell me more about this lake," said Ayda.

I did. While staring into her eyes, I went back over the vision I had, explaining in vivid detail about the flowing river of golden light, the cliff covered in greenery stretching down to an oasis that kept drifting farther and farther away whenever I looked at it, even while pouring sand seemingly filled it. I wanted her to really see that beautiful sapphire-hued lake, and the more I spoke of it, the wider her eyes became. Ayda's gaze seemed to go off into the distance, as though she observed something in another place or time.

"And the strangest thing. I don't believe it was completely a dream." I rolled on my back and pulled the scorpion charm out from under my shirt.

Ayda gasped. "Shaye! Where did you find this?"

"It was just kinda there when I woke up. It felt like I had walked for hours and hours, but after I fell in the lake, I woke back up right at the campsite. I would've thought it all in my head if not for this."

She scooted closer, half on top of me, and brushed her thumb back and forth across the charm. "You most certainly did dream that journey, but sometimes, what is dream and what is real occur together in a place where the..." She searched for a word... "fabric between them is thin. The People of the Sand have welcomed you among them."

"People of the sand?" I ask. "Yeah, they were in the dream or vision or whatever. You're saying they're real?"

"That book you returned to me mentions them. My father was one of those who put a great deal of hope in the old ways. He thought they were real and might be of help to the Saba-al-Bawdi. It was for that reason I sought out that book. It was for him. Well, all of us."

"I hadn't realized it was that important."

She shrugged. "Oh, I'm not so sure it is. Most of what's in there sounds like the sort of things old men talk about late at night around campfires."

"Did it say anything about this?" I dangled the

scorpion between us.

"A few legends. Supposedly, the People of the Sand will help those they have welcomed into their number if called upon. Though it doesn't say exactly what 'help' means. That, and according to the book, those who have gone through their purification ritual are supposedly able to tap some kind of inner power."

"Sounds an awful lot like 'chi' or whatever." I chuckled.

"There's nothing saying the People of the Sand don't exist in other places, or some form of whatever they are." She yawned. "Do you feel more powerful?"

I threaded one arm around her and settled in for sleep. "I haven't really noticed anything too different, though I haven't exactly done much more than ride since."

"Speaking of riding… we should get our rest." She snuggled up beside me and closed her eyes. "Do you know at all where you are going or are you merely following the dog?"

War Daddy, on my right, grunted.

"You know," I muttered, "sometimes, I have the damndest feeling he can understand us."

"Perhaps he can," said Ayda in a sleepy tone.

The dog grunted again, but in a 'settling down for the night' way.

I closed my eyes and tried to let my thoughts drift back to that golden river of light that led me to the waterfall. Had I become part of something greater than most humans ever get to comprehend? I could drive myself crazy wondering if fate brought me to East Sahara or if my encounter with these 'People of the Sand' happened only because I flew out here on a whim. I almost laugh at the thought that I traveled halfway across the globe to return a dog to a blind girl who may only have been a product of my imagination. How low had I fallen that it seemed like a good idea to leave behind everything I knew when I had no solid information to go on? I didn't know for a fact that any child missed this dog. Yet, the vision of her felt like complete truth.

Of course, *now* I'm inclined to think seeing her had been real. But back then? I guess I knew I needed to do something or I'd consume myself with grief and self-loathing until the bottle killed me. The journey had been for me as much as it had been for War Daddy.

I pushed my thoughts back to that image I'd had of her hugging his great furry neck, trying to picture her again. Flashes of a slender girl with light brown skin and long black hair appeared and disappeared. Not a true vision, just my memory of her. I felt myself drifting off... and as I did so, the scenery shifted, and I found myself looking down on what appeared to be a kitchen table in a small dwelling. Somehow, I lay flat against the ceiling. A girl sat alone at the table. Tears dampened her cheeks.

My limited view of the room didn't offer much of any clue as to where she was, though it did suggest she lived in an actual town, not an encampment, a place with at least some electricity. The more I looked around at the two small windows, the more I got the sense of being close to the place. A name drifted across my mind.

"Ameerah," I whispered.

The instant the word passed my lips, the child's eyes snapped open. The shock of her staring straight up at me—and feeling as though she *saw* me there—knocked me out of my vision. The kitchen melted away to the roof of my tent.

"Ameerah," I repeated, a little stronger than a whisper.

War Daddy made a mournful whine.

"Yeah, boy," I said, my emotions a tangle of hope and grief. "I know. You need to go home…"

And—I looked over at Ayda sleeping beside me—so do I.

Chapter Forty-three

After we'd packed up the next morning, I found myself gazing off over the dunes, overcome with a sense of knowing.

Indeed, one particular direction just felt *right*. In fact, it felt *so* right, I stood there like a post staring off into nowhere for long enough that Ayda walked over to check on me.

"What is it? What do you see?" She scanned the clouds for a few seconds. "There is no storm."

A smile formed, though I probably looked more surprised than confident. "It's not a storm I'm seeing—or feeling. Something is pulling me that way." I pointed. "Maybe the People of the Sand help out with GPS."

She chuckled.

"Woof," said War Daddy, and headed in that direction.

I nodded to Kasim who let out a shrill, but short

whistle, a signal to everyone else to depart.

"Well," said Ayda, a note of amusement in her voice. "It seems your intuition is at least aligned with the dog's today."

I walked back to Jake and climbed on while Ayda mounted her camel. Again, we set off into the desert at the meandering pace of unmotivated camels. War Daddy trotted on ahead, seeming a bit annoyed at our languid pace, though it felt adequate to me for reasons I couldn't explain nor dared to question.

For most of the morning, we rode in the low channels between dunes, our direction of travel lining up with the flow of the sand. About an hour before noon, that strange sense of direction pulled me to the right, directly at a fairly steep incline to the mother of all sand dunes. War Daddy felt it as well, and turned toward it.

Jake gave off a grunt of annoyance but didn't protest. When we reached the top of the oversized dune, I gazed down at a sprawling town of mostly plain white buildings. Only about a dozen near the innermost portion stood taller than one story. It appeared reasonably modern, at least for anything I'd so far seen in this country. Here and there, power lines ran on poles, sometimes even using the buildings themselves to keep going down the street. The occasional car sat parked by buildings, but none drove anywhere.

Most surprising of all, a paved road led out of town to the northwest lined with telephone poles on one side.

"Tel Hawah is about six miles away," says Ayda. "Probably the most modern city in all of East Sahara, even more so than the capital El Alalim. Though it's still nothing an American would be used to. This is the town of Nahazeh, a suburb, if you will."

Well, that did at least explain how this girl had a service dog. Her parents likely earned a decent living in the nearby big city. War Daddy headed down, and we followed. Interestingly, he didn't bolt ahead, although I sensed he wanted to. He maintained pace with us, albeit with a constant fidgety impatience and some whining.

"We never go this far east," said Ayda, once we reached the hard-packed dirt beyond the edge of the desert at the base of the dune. "There's only about another hundred miles to the Red Sea."

"Too modern here?" I asked in a—hopefully—humorous tone.

"For some, yes." She nodded. "Others feel our place is in the desert and its energy does not extend into areas 'tamed' by civilization."

"Since you went to the UK, I'm guessing you don't feel that way, or at least you expect to be able to reconnect with it."

She smiled. "It was an interesting experience to see the 'outside world,' but I can't say I miss the constant hurry everyone seemed to be in. As long as I live, I will never understand why people build for themselves a society that consumes their life in cages they call cubicles… or 'day jobs.' Why are people so eager to kill themselves working for the benefit of another?"

I shrugged. "Working for others provides the money needed for food and shelter, and the finer things in life. A modern society also provides conveniences, if one desires, say, a coffee shop on every corner. Some do, and I don't fault them. It can be a nice life. By the way, not all work for others. I worked for myself, and quite enjoyed it."

She studied me. "Tell me you do not prefer it here."

War Daddy turned down another street, and seemed to pick up his pace. I heeled Jake and picked it up as well. So did everyone else.

It's happening...

I said, "When I first stepped off that C-130, I figured I'd be dropping off a dog and going right back. Now, I have no intention of going back."

One thing struck me as odd about Nahazeh. Okay, make that two things: not many people appeared to be out and about despite the size of the place, and two… the ones I did see all tended to glare at us like we didn't belong here. Despite the apparent hostility in their eyes, something told me they meant it more as a warning than a threat. Or maybe they didn't like nomads descending upon their city.

Ayda grinned. "You came all the way here from the US to return a dog to a girl you didn't know, had no information for, and had no way to even know she existed—and you expected it would be a quick trip?"

"In my defense, I hadn't seen the girl until I was in the Cave of Light."

"So you came here with no plan at all?"

"Well, the plan was to follow War Daddy." I stared down at my hands and thought about my arch-enemy: whiskey. The plan had also been to give up the booze. "That said, there's nothing really back there for me. Unless, by some weird circumstance, you wound up back in the States."

She laughed. "Not likely."

War Daddy turned down yet another street, and now his tail whipped back and forth. And I knew why. The area felt right. This was it. Small concrete dwellings lined the street.

"What's with the dog?" asked Ayda.

For an answer, War Daddy dashed across the street, barking happily, and skidded to a stop in front of one of the bigger homes, which wasn't saying much.

"We're here," I said.

"We are?" she asked.

"Yep." I gestured at the dog.

The single story home, made of plain white concrete like most of the town, had a narrow roof extension over the front door, offering shade to some chairs. Tire marks on the ground nearby showed where a car would park. Whatever vehicle belonged there had more than likely taken the girl's father or mother to Tel Hawah for the day. Evidently, not even East Sahara could totally escape from the 'day job.' But the life of a nomad isn't for everyone. I never even considered it might be for me…

I dismounted from Jake, who sat forward on his front legs, and walked up behind the dog who had paused before the home. I took a knee to scratch the fur at his neck. He looked up at me with the same mixture of sorrow and excitement swirling around in my heart. He couldn't stop bouncing with excitement, and barked several more times at the door.

Ayda dismounted as well and moved up beside me.

"If there's a kid in here who belongs to this dog…" She scratched her head.

"Might be time to believe." I gave her hand a squeeze, swallowed the lump in my throat, and rose back to my full height. Gathered myself... and knocked on the heavy front door. "Probably going to need you to do most of the talking."

Ayda nodded.

A thirtyish woman in a reasonably modern dress opened the door after a moment. Her eyebrows began to scrunch together in distrust, and I'm sure the words to send me on my way formed at the tip of her brain—but they didn't make it to her tongue.

War Daddy barked. The way he shook and squirmed, I'm sure he would've plowed straight past her if she didn't block off the entry to the home.

The woman blurted something, then twisted to shout, "Ameerah!" several times before facing me again and saying, "One moment."

Or something that roughly translated to 'wait here a moment.'

She left the door open and darted inside. Rapid Triundic came from within the house, a mixture of that woman's voice and a young girl's. Ayda's eyebrows climbed in surprise. War Daddy trotted straight into the living room.

A barefoot slip of a girl in a plain beige dress rushed down the hallway, tracing her hand on the wall. Other than how she clearly stared into somewhere else, not using her eyes for anything, she appeared healthy and normal—and highly adorable.

"Mama, where?" she repeated a few times in Triundic.

War Daddy barked.

She squealed and rushed forward, heedless of what she might crash into, homing in on his sound. War Daddy darted over to her and guided her to a clear spot of floor where she flopped beside him with her arms around his neck, almost exactly as I'd seen in the vision. The instant his tongue met her cheek, she burst into joyful tears.

And, okay, perhaps I had to wipe my eyes as well.

The mother rushed over to invite us in, though our traveling companions all politely remained outside. Evidently, they expected us to be here a while since they unpacked enough to set up a small campsite beside the house.

Ayda and I sat on the couch while her mother—who introduced herself as Faridah—perched in a somewhat-battered recliner nearby. While Ameerah alternated between squealing and crying with joy, Ayda relayed the story of how I had nearly run War Daddy over back in the US, and wound up deciding on a whim that I really needed to bring him home. Upon my mention of seeing Ameerah in a vision, the child finally released her desperate hug on the dog and pivoted to face me, still sitting back on her heels upon the rug.

Grinning, she spoke with Ayda translating, "I saw you on the ceiling. You told me you found my dog!"

In the midst of Ayda finishing relaying what the child said, the girl leaped up and launched herself into a hug. She *mostly* landed on target and exploded into a barrage of thank-yous, little arms squeezing my neck. The girl made herself breathless trying to say how grateful she was that I'd traveled so far to bring her dog back, and that he meant everything to her, and how sad she'd been ever since he disappeared. When she asked me what happened to him, Faridah gave me a shake of the head.

"Well… he wound up in the United States and…"

Ayda translated as I spoke, but the child blurted, turning her head directly at her, and kept rambling for an insistent while, gesturing over and over at War Daddy.

"She says she knows who took him," offered Ayda in a quiet tone. "And she is afraid that they will do so again."

Faridah bowed her head. She explained that the town of Nahazeh had been essentially taken over by criminal gangs, men who worked for another man who had much power. The term 'crime lord' didn't really translate well, though the moment I muttered 'Sallah' like a swear word, the woman nodded.

She and Ayda conversed for a few minutes. Ameerah scampered off the couch and resumed clinging to War Daddy. Such complete joy radiated from the dog that I felt like a complete heel for being anything but thrilled. I had accomplished exactly what I'd set off to accomplish by coming here, and yet my mood couldn't have been further from happy.

About the only way I could describe my emotional state at that moment would be to compare it to the feeling one gets when bringing a pet to the veterinary clinic for the final time—right before they put them to sleep. On an intellectual level, I knew he belonged here, and reuniting him with Ameerah was the best thing for him. For her as well. For me, not so much. But only a complete piece of shit would take a dog like War Daddy away from a ten-year-old blind girl.

A piece of shit like Sallah.

Again my thoughts returned to wondering how

exactly an animal as fierce and deadly as War Daddy turned out to be captured. It didn't seem likely at all that he had allowed it as he had evidently done when Ahmed's people abducted us together. No, there, I had a distinct feeling he *wanted* to be taken so my path would again cross Ayda's. Of course, that amounted to total insanity, but after everything I'd seen here, I couldn't deny it. This dog appeared to know what my soul needed. Maybe even what Ayda's needed.

And now, he once again protected the child who had loved him before I even knew he existed.

She whispered to him, and by all that lived and breathed, I swore that dog murmured and yipped in response, and the girl reacted as though he spoke to her. Of course, she could have very well been pretending, as children are wont to do. But… yeah.

"Shaye," said Ayda in a gentle tone, distracting me from my forlorn stare at my no-longer dog. She leaned close, talking low so the girl couldn't hear us. "This town is overrun with Sallah's men. The police do nothing because they are corrupt or too afraid. His men take whatever they want from the stores or homes here, do whatever they want to the people. It sounds like they are living in a completely different country, one run by a military junta with a cruel warlord."

"They will take him again," said Ameerah. "Please don't let them take War Daddy again."

Damn. Kid had good ears.

"You know," I said, leaning back and rubbing a

finger back-and-forth across my lip. "Maybe it's about time someone had a talk with this Sallah. That whole wanting to kill me thing I could ignore, but, he's gonna take the dog again."

"Do you think so?" asked Ayda.

"No idea. I'm just saying that as an excuse to convince myself to do something rash, impetuous, reckless, dangerous, and foolish."

"Like fly across the globe to bring a dog home?" she asked with a smile.

"Yeah. Something like that. Half-baked ideas seem to be working for me lately." I took her hand and kissed it, fairly sure Faridah would disapprove of us locking lips in her house right in front of her. "And I can't let that man take this little girl's dog… again."

Ayda raised an eyebrow. "What do you propose to do?"

"Oh, I figured I'll just go ask him nicely to leave this town alone and stop using dogs to mule drugs into the US."

She blinked, calling me a fool with her eyes.

"There will probably be guns involved." I winked. "Besides. As soon as he sees reason, I don't have to worry about my presence being a threat to the Saba-al-Bawdi."

"Hmm." Ayda pondered a moment, exchanging a few words with Faridah. "She tells me they occupy an abandoned military base about a fifteen-minute drive from here. It is also where Sallah lives."

"Excellent."

"You're serious?" she asked, blinking again. "You're suggesting we go attack this man?"

"He gutted my dog," I said, gesturing at him. "Well, *her* dog. And yes, I'm serious. Ill-planned commando raids on drug kingpins living in desert strongholds is a hobby of mine. I usually work the raids in-between root canals."

She laughed.

"Seriously, what do you think?" I asked. "Am I being totally crazy or can I pull this off?"

"*You* cannot pull this off, but *we* might." She nodded matter-of-factly. "I will talk to the others. If they are willing to join you, we shall rid East Sahara of Sallah. However, I would suggest a quieter approach."

"Perfect. Sneak in, deal with him, sneak back out, home in time for lunch."

"I am concerned that you are not taking this seriously."

I leaned close, an arm around her. "I need something to distract myself from leaving War Daddy here and never seeing him again. Being a wise-ass is how I cope with nerves. Not really sure why this seems like a great idea, but it does seem like the right thing to do."

"Perhaps you have inspiration." Ayda picked at the scorpion pendant through my shirt. "Promise me you will not do anything foolish."

"What do you call a washed-up dentist hopping on a military cargo plane to return a dog home halfway across the world?"

She smirked. "Promise me you will not do anything *else* foolish, especially when it could kill you. I happen to like you."

I took her hand in both of mine, looked her straight in the eyes, and said, "I promise."

Chapter Forty-four

Once Faridah finished telling us about how Sallah and his men had made this town their personal playground—everything from extorting 'protection' money from the residents to young women sometimes going missing—we migrated out to the backyard.

By that time, the men had taken care of the camels, setting them up with water and food, and joined us. We discussed how best to handle the 'Sallah situation' while Ameerah and War Daddy played. If ever anyone asked me what true joy looked like, I'd describe this child being reunited with her dog.

And yeah, I still felt like a bastard for not being totally thrilled with the situation. Mostly out of selfishness. I'd formed a bond with that dog, too, dammit. But, this is where he belonged and my entire reason for coming here was to bring him back to this kid.

Mission accomplished as they say. But... ugh.

Then again, the Universe might have had another reason to bring me here, to this place. For Ayda, perhaps. To do away with Sallah and his gang... definitely.

I had a dog once years ago as a kid. Technically, he had been my parents' before I happened. I was around seven or eight when he finally died, and I think that grief had something to do with why I never had another pet. Or maybe I'd just been so busy and absorbed with school, dentistry, material possessions, marriage, trying to succeed, I never made time for anything else. My former hygienist, Lee, once told me it's almost like a mental condition for pet people. Losing a pet is so horrible there's this small period where you can't imagine getting another one because of the inevitable loss, but then you see that kitten or puppy and you forget entirely about what's going to happen in ten years or so.

And as I sat there watching War Daddy fetch a ball and bring it right back to Ameerah's little outstretched hand, I mostly felt like I'd lost my dog. Though her occasional bright giggle eased my guilt.

Her father, Bahir, returned while we sat out back socializing. The girl, clinging to War Daddy for guidance, ran over to him and chattered so fast I think even Ayda had trouble understanding her. The man soon understood what transpired and offered his hearty thanks.

"My daughter has been a ghost of a person without that dog," said Bahir in reasonable English. "You have done us a great service."

"Eh… just something I had to do."

"No, no…" He smiled, patting my shoulder. "Turning him in at a shelter would've been something anyone would've done. Not many would have journeyed as you have."

I hooked my thumbs in my pockets and chuckled at the ground. He had no way to know the true extent of the journey I took, at least from a metaphysical perspective. "It had to happen."

Again Bahir clapped me on the shoulder. "You are a remarkable man, Doctor Shaye."

"I keep telling him that but he doesn't seem to believe me," muttered Ayda with a wink.

Bahir invited us all to stay for dinner, and we had the East Sahara version of a backyard barbecue, though the food was cooked inside. Still, it made me think of a grand affair due to the ten of us plus the family. Humayd, Jamil, and Gadi entertained Ameerah with stories of the desert while Ayda and I discussed our plan. Bahir appeared simultaneously nervous about the idea of a direct attack on Sallah, even as he gave off hope. According to him, this town had been miserable for the past eight years, and he would not shed any tears over the man's death... or any of his men. Unfortunately, Bahir also informed us that Sallah had 'friends' in the East Saharan military. This, of course, translated to bribes. And a lot of firepower.

"So whatever we do, it has to be quiet, and fast," I said. "Is this guy likely to call in the Army on us?"

Bahir shook his head. "His arrangement with them is not like that. More that they will turn a blind eye to whatever he does... and provide him with weapons and equipment."

I nodded. "All right."

"We should move under cover of night," said Dawud. "And first observe and measure what we are up against."

"Yeah." I tapped my fingers on the thin metal folding table, still littered with plates and empty cups. "I can't ask any of you to do anything suicidal. If it's too much, we fall back and maybe we try to catch him when he travels."

"Sallah is…" Bahir waved his hand around, searching for a word. "Paranoid. He does not often leave his stronghold. And when he does, he usually has a dozen or more men with him and an armored car."

"Mercedes," said Ayda. "Like the one they took me in, only bulletproof."

"Well, let's go have a look at this fort. It's dark." I sighed and glanced at War Daddy.

As if sensing my imminent departure, he nuzzled Ameerah, stood, and padded over to me, resting his head in my lap.

"Hey, boy." I scratched behind both his ears. "Well, you're home. I guess this is that moment I'd been trying not to think too much about."

He licked at my hand.

"I know. This is where you belong. I always knew that but it's different to be at that moment... and this moment. You're my friend, and I'll never forget you."

Ayda petted War Daddy's head, smiling.

I pressed my hand down on top of hers. "I'd like to think fate somehow put us together for a reason, and I'm pretty sure you led me to the woman my soul needed to be with."

War Daddy flattened his ears and stared up at me with a 'certainly took you long enough' expression—or maybe it meant 'those damn leopard claws hurt.'

Ameerah crawled over and knelt beside the dog, her arms wrapped around him. "Why are you sad, Doctor Shaye?"

I slid off my chair, took a knee beside the dog, and hugged him like he was minutes from death. I'd have answered her question, but if I opened my mouth, I probably would've cried.

"You have a special friend in this dog, Ameerah," said Ayda. "In the short time they spent together, the two have become quite close. The way you felt when he was taken from you is how Doctor Shaye feels now. But, he knows War Daddy and you need to be together."

"Yeah," I muttered, trying to sound as cool and collected as possible. Managing one word about reached my limit.

"I understand." Ameerah said with Ayda translating. The girl scooted around and hugged me. "Thank you for bringing War Daddy home. I was so sad without him."

Words wouldn't come out. I managed a nod, patted her on the back, and let out a long sigh once she released the hug. She resumed clinging to War Daddy. The dog locked stares with me, and his eyes gave off a sense of gratitude mixed with relief and frustration.

"Yeah, yeah," I said, patting him on the head. "If I'd have been faster rushing that Mercedes, you wouldn't have gotten all clawed up."

He made a 'Murff' noise and licked my face, a note of 'don't worry about it' in his body language.

"Okay, well." I scratched him behind his ears again and stood. "We better get on with this or I'm going to sit here for another six days."

Everyone chuckled.

Bahir and Faridah exchanged a glance, gave me a pointed look, and whispered at each other. Faridah said something that made Bahir's eyebrows go up in a 'that's a damn good idea' sort of way, though neither one of them said anything to me.

Hmm. Wonder what that was about. Since neither approached me, I figured they were planning some kind of celebration if we actually managed to survive this.

For the second time in my life, I had a 'what the hell am I doing?' moment.

Chapter Forty-five

We headed out into the desert, having left most of our basic supplies with Bahir's family.

The men had a mix of AK47s and SKS semi-automatics among them. Seeing the weapons lit a fire of anxiety in my gut, but not enough to make me back off. War Daddy had gone through a vicious mauling to make sure my life intersected Ayda's. The least I could do for him would be to safeguard the family he loved.

Light and stealthy, the camels took us into the desert west of Nahazeh. Driving would've been faster, but Sallah's people would've seen (or heard) us coming easily. I couldn't tell if I'd been in the desert long enough to acclimate to starlight or if my new relationship with this People of the Sand thing had anything to do with it, but despite it being the middle of the night I had no trouble seeing.

In a paradoxical way, it almost felt like headlights would've made it *harder* to navigate. And, of course, a moving light source in the desert would've been visible for many miles.

Within ten minutes of leaving town, once the—albeit feeble—glow of its few street lights faded behind us, the distant glow of the former military fort became quite obvious up ahead. Best I figured, it sat about four or five miles away. We'd left the true desert behind, and no longer had the cover of dunes to hide behind. The land here consisted mostly of flat hard-packed sand with a liberal dotting of green scrub and some gnarled-looking wood-like bushes about waist high. I couldn't tell if they remained alive or had died.

Having such an easy time *finding* this place made me a little nervous since nothing is ever that easy. Though, we hadn't passed any point of no return yet. Our mission still consisted of scouting.

Ayda took the lead, guiding us to the right instead of directly at the old base. I didn't quite understand the move right away but trusted her enough to keep quiet. Eventually, I caught on that she headed for an elevated ridge a few hundred yards away from the fort that would give us a good view.

Upon reaching the base of the hill, we all dismounted. Jamil and Kasim remained with the camels to guard them and keep them from wandering off. The rest of us walked up to the ridge and passed around the two pairs of binoculars the tribe owned.

A fourteen-foot wall made of the same white concrete as most of the homes in the nearby town surrounded a large building, two tiny ones, and a sizable tarmac that held four black Mercedes SUVs, a half-dozen battered pickup trucks, and a pair of large box trucks. Strong lights glowed from the farthest-left three windows on the biggest building. With the binoculars, I peered in on a room full of chemistry equipment. Looked like about a quarter of the ground floor held the lab where they processed the various drugs.

This installation had clearly been abandoned by the military for a while before Sallah moved in, as most of the buildings had crumbled. Numerous places where cracks caused concrete to fall away exposed reinforcing re-bars inside. Even some graffiti marked the cement, suggesting the local youth had been able to walk in and out before it became the hub of a criminal enterprise.

Only a handful of sentries moved around outside, suggesting they had become relatively complacent under the amount of fear Sallah commanded among the locals. I figured they wouldn't expect a direct attack. Also, the low number of guards made sneaking in feel all the more possible.

"He is here," said Ayda. "Third Mercedes from the left. It is his."

I looked at it. Though it appeared identical to the rest at this distance, it sat an inch or two lower on its suspension, no doubt from the weight of the bulletproofing. "Good. Do you guys think the old cutting off the head of the snake will work?"

"That would definitely free you from Sallah's vendetta, and most likely help the people of Naha-zeh," said Ayda. "But there are always others eager for power."

"His men will probably fight for the scraps of his empire," said Dawud, his words translated by Ayda. "I don't expect we'll eradicate the entire drug trade in East Sahara, but people will be much less fearful of multiple small groups than one as organized as Sallah's base of operations."

"So... do you still wish to do this?" asked Ayda.

I scanned the fort for a moment more, then heaved a resigned sigh. "Yeah. He's gonna take the dog again. Let's go ask him not to... unless you think this is too foolish."

We conferred for a few minutes, discussing how best to proceed. Abir identified a likely point of entry along the rear corner. Both he and Dawud also served as scouts and spies for the tribe and knew what they were talking about. Apparently, these two had spent many years perfecting the art of stealth. Not everyone in the Saba-al-Bawdi focused entirely on hand-to-hand fighting.

Abir led the way down the facing side of the ridge. Jamil and Kasim would remain with the camels, both to protect them and either bail us out or return to the tribe for additional help in the event the second ridiculous idea of my life didn't work out the way I hoped.

Really, how hard could it be to sneak into an

abandoned military base, take out a drug lord, and sneak back out? And yeah, I knew a thirtysomething dentist had no business doing anything like this, but for reasons I didn't understand, it felt completely possible. I even found myself noticing how the shadows thickened in places and knowing to stick to them; picking up on noises within the compound like breathing, the rattle of a rifle, footsteps on dirt.

All stuff I should in no way be able to pick up on.

I fidgeted with the scorpion amulet as we tucked up behind the outer wall, hoping the People of the Sand would bring me luck, and entertaining the idea that perhaps Ayda had been right and I had developed some inexplicable supernatural senses.

Figured if such a thing existed, I'd damn sure need it soon.

We followed the wall to the end corner, where Abir climbed over it like a wraith, using missing bits of concrete as places to grab and step. He perched at the top, peering over for a few seconds before jumping down. Amid a billowing flutter of cloth, the soft *thump* of feet hitting the ground accompanied a muffled gurgle.

Dawud went up the wall next. He, too, paused at the top, but only long enough to wave for us to follow. I moved without giving it much thought, grabbing and stepping as they had. Though I probably didn't flow up it like a spirit, I'd like to think I didn't make *too* much noise. Once at the top,

I spotted the source of the gurgle. Abir had ambushed a patrolling man, likely grabbing him from behind and plunging a knife into his heart. Wow, I felt nothing for the dead man.

I had my 9mm to back up my sword. Ayda had only a sword on her, so when Abir handed me the dead man's AK, I passed it on to her. The men all gave me various degrees of 'wow really' expressions, as if giving a woman a firearm transcended some other level of 'things that should not be done in the desert.' Then again, Ayda was their leader, and she already carried a blade, so they let it go with no more reaction than raised eyebrows.

"I hope you're not planning on us needing these," whispered Ayda while checking the weapon over. The ease with which she handled it caught me off guard as it did the other men. "One loud shot and we will have many more problems than Sallah."

I shook my head. "My preference is to stay quiet."

After dragging the body behind a stack of old crates, we hunkered down in the shadow of the wall and moved one at a time across about thirty feet of open tarmac to the inky darkness behind the largest building. We approached the side opposite the brightly lit lab. Farran and I were the last to make the trip, however, we needed to wait for a sentry on the roof to walk away before we moved out from behind the crates.

I led the way around the building, and stopped short at the sight waiting for me. Ayda almost ran into me, I'd stopped so fast. A long row of kennel cages stood against the wall, holding perhaps twenty dogs of various breeds, though fortunately, no more East Saharan Shepherds. The two of us froze like kids caught with our hands in the cookie jar. If even one of those dogs started to bark, we'd be done.

Ayda gasped, grabbed my arm, and squeezed. She clearly expected the dogs to erupt in a boatload of noise. The men, confused, stacked up behind her halfway around the corner.

I raised a hand at the dogs. "Easy," I whispered. "Stay quiet, okay?"

They shifted around in their cages, eyeing me.

"Calm," I whispered, wishing for all I had that the dogs understood me. "I'll get you out of there, but you have to stay quiet and calm, okay?"

As if by magic, every single dog continued to stare at me, not one of them so much as gruffing.

"What's going on?" whispered Ayda.

"I dunno," I replied. "Think the dogs know I'm going to get them out of here so they're trusting us."

We hurriedly opened all the cages. And without so much as a yip, the dogs zoomed off across the tarmac, squeezing one after the next through a broken hole in the wall... and were gone. Poof, just like that.

Mahmoud muttered something. I assumed it roughly translated to "Well shit, now I've seen everything." Or something to that effect.

A canine whimper emanated from a steel door

beyond the last cage. Perhaps reacting a bit too hastily, I rushed for it and barged in. Two men struggled to hold down a medium-sized dog while a third tried (and presently failed) to force it to swallow a plastic packet about the size of a half-banana. I couldn't help but notice the guy with the drug packet didn't have an index finger on his left hand.

Son of a bitch.

Chapter Forty-six

The two men holding the dog blinked at me in shock, but before either could do so much as yell, I tackled the man with the drugs.

My team rushed in behind me and cut the other two down with swords. Meanwhile, I rolled back and forth on the floor with the man I'd leapt on, trying to keep him from pulling a handgun off his belt. No sooner had I rolled onto my back with him on top of me—attempting a rather lame choke hold —Abir swooped in and knifed the man in the chest. He gurgled, twitched, and went still in a few seconds.

Though I'd taken a few lives the night of the attack on the camp, *holding* a man down while he dies felt entirely different. Maybe it would bother me later, but this guy might have even been the one to force-feed War Daddy whatever drugs had been cut out of him.

By the time I got to my feet, the dog had already run off.

"We will have been heard," said Farran, wiping blood from his cutlass. "Let us be quick."

I'd spent enough time in the Navy Reserve to have a general idea of the layout for places like this. Fair bet a self-important jackass like Sallah would install himself in the base commander's office. I headed across this storage room to the only door, which led to a corridor. Fortunately, no one had yet come to investigate the shouting, so I jogged down the hall to the stairwell, the others close behind.

Once upstairs, I hurried from door to door, peering in. One office had a handful of computers, but no people. The next appeared empty. A locked door looked enough like a storage closet that I ignored it. Probably full of guns or something to be secured like that.

A pale blue door at the end of the corridor felt like it called me. So, being the overly careful, thoughtful man I am, I headed straight to it, peeked inside—and locked stares with Sallah. Or who I assumed was Sallah.

Not to mention his ten or so buddies.

Oops.

"You surprise me, American," said the man who could be Sallah, speaking in clear English. "First, you interfere with my operation, then you have the nerve to disrupt a vital financial channel from one of my associates… now you stroll right into my office? Are you trying to collect the bounty on yourself?"

Nothing like staring Death in his cold bony eye sockets to give a man a giant pair of balls.

I shoved the door open and walked in like I owned the place. "You have a real odd way of phrasing things. 'Interfere with my operation' for being rude enough not to let your men murder me and steal my dog? 'Disrupting a financial channel' did that refer to the dog fighting or the human trafficking while I tried my damndest not to be abducted?" I hold up a hand. "Wait. Don't answer that, I really don't want to know. You're talking like I walked into your life one day and decided to piss in your Cheerios. If your idiots had kept their hands to themselves, I wouldn't be here right now." I rubbed my chin. "Or maybe I would. There's still that whole mess in Nahazeh... a mess you created."

Sallah's cheeks reddened with rage. For a moment, I thought his eyeballs would pop straight out of his head. "Before I have you shot like the dog you are, I wish to know what you expected to accomplish by coming here—other than hastening your death."

Ayda and the others hovered in the hall. Given all ten of Sallah's men stared at *me,* I entertained the hope that my allies retained the element of surprise.

"Well, I figured you might be a reasonable sort of man, so I came here to ask you to leave Nahazeh alone, stop abusing dogs... and oh yeah, it would be really nice of you to get out of the whole 'crime lord' business. Maybe open an electronics store or a coffee shop?"

For a second, I almost thought I'd succeed in killing him via anger-induced heart attack. Veins swelled in his forehead, his eyeballs appeared to inflate even more, and he shook, too pissed off to even form words.

One of the thugs laughed, though I couldn't tell if he found what I said amusing or simply thought me the biggest idiot he'd ever seen. Or if he even understood English.

"Ahh, didn't think so. Oh, wait. I forgot to say 'please.'" With that, I whipped out my 9mm.

I managed a hasty shot on my way to dive behind a giant metal desk, expecting a hail of gun-fire. Sallah shouted a mixture of rage and pain, English and Triundic. If I hit him, it only grazed. Ayda and the others rushed in screaming war cries, and opened fire on the thugs. Caught off guard, most of the enemy still fired into the desk I hid behind.

The stink of cordite filled the air in seconds.

Ayda dove for cover beside me, the other tribe-smen behind us scattered to either side—everyone wasted ammo while focusing more on *not* being shot than hitting anything. A few men cried out in pain, likely winged by errant ricochets.

"This desk isn't gonna last long," I muttered, pointing at a hole in the sheet metal.

"You are not a good assassin," said Ayda. "Dentist, yes. Assassin, no."

I grinned. Rifles boomed and clattered from every direction. Empty, smoking brass rolled by on the floor. Somewhere under the din, Sallah shouted in raging Triundic. I caught the word for testicles, and didn't really want to know where he was going with that.

With a grunt, I popped up over the desk, spotted Sallah hiding behind a cement column maybe twenty feet farther into the room, and fired twice at him, spraying him in the face with fragments of concrete. It gave me an opening to move, so I jumped up and over the desk and ran to another three-foot-square concrete pillar, and hunkered down behind it. Narrow, but—unlike the desk—bullets couldn't go through it.

Ayda fired rapidly at a group of men on the right side of the room, taking at least two out. Yeah, she made a helluva leader.

Sallah and I traded pistol shots for a few seconds that felt like minutes.

Infuriated, he ducked out of sight. I eased around the side of the support structure, cringing when another bullet powdered concrete in front of my face. Ducking back, I pivoted and shot twice at the guy pointing an AK at me. He collapsed out of sight behind a row of filing cabinets, clutching a wound in the neck. Mercy, that had to hurt. I shifted my aim back to Sallah's hiding place and all but screamed when his hand came up, lobbing a grenade at me.

Time seemed to slow down as I stared at the

twisting, oblong bomb coming toward me. Without even thinking, I rushed out from behind the column, grabbed the grenade out of midair like plucking an apple from a branch, and hurled it out the nearest window.

Sallah didn't even react to me until I'd rounded the column behind which he'd taken cover and put my 9mm to his forehead.

Boom.

A layer of dust basted off the walls. The floor shook. Crap on desks fell over, and a peppering of shrapnel clanked and clattered at the wall.

No, my gun didn't do that—the grenade outside did. My gun went *click*. Hmm.

I do think Sallah might've stained his underwear though. Loud bangs from anything while a handgun is pressed against one's forehead tends to be mildly alarming.

"Misfire." I said, shrugging. "Must be a bad round."

With him staring at me, stunned, I racked the slide to chamber a new bullet, but it locked back, empty. My very last bullet and it didn't go off. Figures. The odd silence surrounding us made me glance left and right. All of Sallah's men lay dead or too wounded to continue fighting. Gadi clutched his shot shoulder, though the wound didn't appear life-threatening. Humayd had taken a graze to the left thigh, though he largely ignored it. I suppose after the slash he sustained during the raid on our camp, this didn't hurt much at all. My friends all looked at me with strange expressions

Sallah snapped out of his shock, though his cheeks remained a few shades paler than usual…. He grabbed a saber from the desk and went to swing it at me, but flinched when I threw my empty 9mm at his face. That bought me enough time to draw my own sword. He lunged in with a hard downward slash that I parried easily. He expertly leaned back to spare his throat from my counterattack. Not bad at all. Turned out, his sword was more than for just show. The man had been trained.

Either because of how close I stood to him or out of curiosity to see how it went, neither Ayda nor any of the others shot Sallah over the course of us trading several swings. His cutlass outweighed my rapier, so I tried to dodge more than cross swords with him. I also had no interest in 'pulling an Ayda' and toying with him. I wanted this over as fast as possible.

The sixth time our blades bounced off each other, I saw my opening. Although skilled, he wasn't a collegiate foiling champion. Lame as that sounded, it had taught me to constantly seek out my opponent's weaknesses. There. He stumbled when I feinted low. A rare misstep? I didn't know. We crossed swords and circled. As we did so, I feinted low again and he staggered again reaching down to block.

I lunged forward and pierced his thigh. He cried out and stumbled back. He looked down at the wound, then at me—and hurled his sword at like a javelin. I knocked it aside as he bolted across the room—or tried to. The limp slowed him down, and a few of my friends' bullets sparking on the floor at his boot heels. He jumped out the same window I lobbed the grenade through earlier.

Humayd and Farran ran to the window and fired a few times. They turned back and spoke rapidly.

"They say he's pinned down behind a truck, Shaye. They will shoot him if he moves," said Ayda.

"Great." I put my sword away, grabbed the 9mm—as well as a dead guy's AK47—and hurried to the door.

I holstered the pistol while running down the hall to the stairs and making my way as best as I could estimate to the closest door to where Sallah leapt. A man popped out of a doorway, raising an SKS at me, but I fed him two rounds before he could fire. On the way past the room, I nearly yelled out in disbelief at the sight of a rocket launcher lying right out in the open on a table.

What the hell? Oh, right… 'friends' in the military.

A ripple of gunfire went off somewhere in the distance, probably Humayd and Farran trading bullets with more of Sallah's men outside.

With Ayda, Abir, Dawud, Gadi, and Mahmoud behind me, I rounded another corner and sprinted to the door at the end, certain it led to the outside. I whipped it open—and stopped short, staring at a row of about thirty guys, all with rifles pointed at me.

Sallah staggered to his feet and limped out from behind a shot-up box truck, grinning at me despite blood surging out his nose and his thigh. He sauntered over to take a position at the middle of his thugs, grinning at me. "You are not going to die slow, my friend. It would enrage me to see you die a quick death. Give up, accept the fate you deserve, and I shall let the girl leave unharmed."

A rifle shot rang out *right* next to my ear.

"I am not *the girl!*" shouted Ayda.

Unfortunately, her shot didn't kill Sallah. I barely had time to notice the spurt of blood from his shoulder before grabbing Ayda and diving for cover beside the doorway, narrowly avoiding a barrage of bullets flooding the corridor.

"The nerve!" said Ayda, fuming. "And no I didn't believe him for a second. He would have killed me, too. Or worse."

Our guys ran deeper into the corridor, taking up firing positions at two corners, and throwing enough ammo out the doorway to keep the thirty or so men outside from storming in after us.

"This isn't going to end well," said Ayda, a second before an explosion of concrete dust fell on us from a bullet penetrating the wall.

I glanced up at it. "Shit. Nope. Sorry. My fault. Stupid idea."

"Equally my fault for going along with it."

I squeezed her hand. "I'd do it all over again to be with you."

She pushed my hand onto my chest, over the scorpion pendant. "Legends say that—"

We both flinched at a rain of dust. Automatic fire outside continued punishing the wall. Fortunately, as an old military installation, I'm sure they put in some armor plating, or we'd have been aerated already.

I clutched it. "Yeah… If there's any truth to the People of the Sand being there to provide help when asked… this is me asking."

A noticeable glimmer danced across the scorpion's sapphire eyes.

Ayda blinked. "Did you see that?"

I nodded. I had. Son of a bitch... I had.

Outside, a man shrieked in agony.

Focused gunfire on the doorway ceased, though the sound of shooting didn't. Men shouted a mixture of war cries, terrified screams, and painful wails. After a few seconds of no bullets coming in, I risked peeking around the doorjamb, which had been shredded.

Eight figures in long, dark red robes trimmed in gold, dashed about in a graceful but deadly ballet of swordsmanship. Swords of mirror-polished silver gleamed in the moonlight, cutting down Sallah's men like farmers harvesting sugar cane. Wherever bullets struck them, their bodies disintegrated into swirling clouds of sand, but reformed an instant later, not even slowing them down.

Next to me, Ayda stared with wide-eyed awe.

Still on the ground clutching his wounded

shoulder, Sallah dragged himself away, heading for the row of Mercedes SUVs. Normally, I'd probably have an issue shooting an unarmed guy crawling away on the ground… but Sallah. Letting him slink away would only cause much greater problems down the road. Men like him don't take losing gracefully. And, after everything he'd done to those dogs, I don't have the least bit of pity for him.

I raised my rifle. "This is for War Daddy."

Ayda fired nearly the same instant I did. Sallah slumped over dead, two 7.62mm holes in the middle of his chest.

"And that's for me," she grumbled, a rare moment of pain on her face.

Though I freed her, and the other women, from Ahmed before anything worse than being abducted happened to her, she no doubt carried a few mental scars from the experience of being treated like livestock. I threaded an arm around her and held her tight to my side. She raised her head high with poise befitting the leader of the Saba-al-Bawdi, but didn't pull away. Later, when we had a tent to ourselves, I would comfort her.

The People of the Sand did not pursue those who abandoned their weapons and fled. With the threat at an end, they assembled in a line, facing us.

I bowed my head in gratitude.

All eight of them nodded in acknowledgment… and blew away on the breeze.

Okay, wow. I would process that later, if I could.

"We are finished here," said Ayda.

"Almost," I said. "Be right back."

I hurried inside, waving the men to follow me to that one room I'd seen on the way through. I grabbed one of the rocket launchers, gestured for the others to collect the remaining three, as well as two boxes of rifle ammo. Hey, take supplies where we can get them, right?

As soon as I walked outside with the thing over my shoulder, Ayda did the math. Rockets plus a room full of volatile chemicals equaled a real kick in the balls to the drug trade of East Sahara.

"Wait," she said. "Give me a few minutes."

"All right. Need a hand?"

"Nah."

She darted back inside. The men and I collected all the dropped rifles, a couple handguns, and two swords, tossing everything in the back of the first pickup truck with keys tucked under the sun visor. A short while later, Ayda reappeared with two young women who might have been eighteen. Of course, Sallah would have had his pick of the trafficked girls.

"Shit," I muttered. "I should've thought to search for prisoners."

She held up a big lockbox. "This should come in handy as well. Most of his money is probably in various banks, but this is still pretty hefty."

"Cool." I raised the launcher at the glowing windows. "Are we sure there's no people or dogs left alive in there?"

"Yes. I checked everywhere."

"Even that locked closet?" I asked.

She patted her AK. "I brought my lock pick. Opened right up. Just computer equipment."

"Okay." I looked around at my friends. "Might want to step back a little. Or a lot."

Since none of the men knew how to drive, Ayda took the young women with her in the pickup truck and headed back to Nahazeh. The others gave me a healthy bit of distance, and I squeezed the trigger, lobbing the ungainly projectile clean through the window and into the chem lab.

The desert lit up with a dazzling display of fireworks.

Chapter Forty-seven

As best I figure, we'd made it back to the town a little past two in the morning.

A handful of locals still lingered at the western limits, probably trying to figure out what had exploded way off in the distance. No one paid us any attention beyond casual glances as we passed. So as not to disturb Bahir and his family, we all slept in our campsite beside his house—after I did my best to attend to Gadi and Humayd's injuries.

Gadi had suffered a through-and-through to the shoulder, which fortunately missed bone. It had to hurt like hell though, as he'd been sweating profusely since we left the old fort. I suggested this town probably had a clinic of some sort, or at the minimum, we'd go to Tel Hawah which would definitely have a hospital. Humayd's leg had suffered a grazing wound that really did need stitches, but I didn't have anything of the sort with me, so we made do with a tight bandage.

We awoke next morning to Ameerah and War Daddy playing in the backyard. Faridah emerged from the house soon after we stirred, offering food, water, and coffee. Bahir had evidently taken the day off from his job with the power company in Tel Hawah, as he joined us for breakfast.

Over our meal, we explained to Bahir that Sallah was no more. We did leave out any mention of the People of the Sand. War Daddy sat nearby, giving me this look of pride that I'd managed to keep myself intact without him there to cover for me.

As it turned out, one of the young women had been abducted from Nahazeh only a week earlier. Her father still wore the bandages from his effort to stop Sallah's men from taking her straight out of their home.

After a quick meal, I insisted on packing Gadi and Humayd in the pickup truck, and driving them to Tel Hawah. I'd planned to go with a story about thieves attacking our camp to explain the bullet wounds, but the medical staff there didn't even ask... nor did they involve any sort of law enforcement. Guess I'm still too used to American ways.

It took a few hours for them to clean up and stitch the wounds. Gadi appeared grateful for the painkillers, though couldn't walk too well on his own after. Humayd and I ushered him back out to the truck, and we arrived back in Nahazeh a bit after four in the afternoon.

I knew right away that something was up.

Ayda wouldn't look at me. Though she didn't seem upset at all. She tried to pretend nothing at all was unusual, which only made me more suspicious. After helping Gadi to his temporary bed in the next room, I sauntered over to her and wrapped my arms around her from behind.

"Are you going to tell me why you're avoiding eye contact," I asked, smiling.

"Perhaps," she said in an amused tone.

"Something's up."

"Woof." War Daddy trotted over and rubbed his head against my leg.

Ameerah poked her head out of the house door and said, "Hi, Doctor Shaye," and ducked back inside.

I scratched War Daddy under his jaw. "Hey boy. I know… I know… Can't stay here forever. I'm sure your family wants their space back."

He heaved a low, groaning dog-sigh that I took to mean his heart had become as heavy as mine at the thought of our parting ways.

"We've been through it and then some, huh, boy?" I ruffled his fur. "But this is where you belong, and you've shown me where I belong. All that old stuff I used to value, well, it doesn't mean a damn thing." I put an arm around Ayda. "She is all I need."

The soft scuff of sandals approached behind me, but at the slowness of the pace and the absence of any violent feelings in the air, I didn't bother looking back, instead trying to prolong the time I got to spend with War Daddy.

"Doctor Shaye," said Ameerah.

I smiled at the dog. He grinned as well, tongue lolling out to the side. As sad as he might be that our paths must go in different directions, he seemed even happier to be reunited with her. I couldn't begrudge either one of them that happiness, especially not after finding Ayda.

"Yes?" I asked, turning to look back.

The child stood beside her father, who had guided her over to me. Her toes gripped the carpet with childish glee, matching the humongous smile on her face. At first, I thought she clutched a big plush teddy bear—until it moved.

"He wants to stay with you," said Ameerah.

"Is that a…" I blinked in disbelief at a minuscule version of War Daddy. A puppy. He hadn't even grown into his fur yet, so he looked like a giant cotton ball with eyes.

War Daddy held his head high and barked.

The puppy yipped in response.

"It seems our dog was rather friendly with another shepherd who lives on the far side of Nahazeh," said Bahir. "He is the last of the litter. Would always hide whenever people came to look. But not this time."

"Almost like he waited for you," said Ayda, giving me a playful elbow nudge.

Ameerah held the puppy out to me. "You love War Daddy, too," she said with Ayda translating.

"Your eyes work, but you still need a dog to love."

I cradled the tiny version of War Daddy, who promptly licked my nose.

Ayda practically melted at the sight of him. Surely she'd seen them return with the pup while I'd been at the hospital. That explained why she couldn't look me in the eye—she'd not have been able to resist telling me about the surprise waiting for me.

Faridah walked up and stood beside her daughter, all three of them smiling at me. War Daddy sat in front of Ameerah, who squatted to hug him.

My heart felt like a tractor-trailer ran it over. Going from near death experience last night to the loss of War Daddy to the shock of a puppy left me stunned.

After a minute or so of me not saying a word, Ayda nudged me. "What shall we name him?"

I stared into his brilliant golden eyes, glanced at the dog who'd led me halfway around the world, then back at my new little buddy. "War Baby."

Chapter Forty-eight

There is something fairly specific to be said about nomadic desert life—I never have to worry about a puppy crapping all over the nice new carpet.

While War Baby ran around playing with several children, I worked to set up my tent. For the next week or two, the Saba-al-Bawdi would stay among the trees of the Qadeith Oasis and it's glimmering blue lake, the third largest in East Sahara. It sat roughly at the midpoint of the desert, occupying about three square miles, so it made for a major trading stop among the nomadic groups.

I'd gotten into a fairly regular routine of providing wandering dentistry services whenever we made stops like this. The money Ayda liberated from Sallah's office paid for some almost-modern equipment, though I didn't get anything too bulky to carry around or too delicate to survive being out in the desert. Granted, the supplier in Tel Hawah hardly had the same sort of cutting-edge gear I could get in the States, but I didn't exactly see myself ever going back there.

Yeah, I had messed up. A couple of lawsuits still hounded me back there, plus the house. I still had some money in the bank, but felt so little attachment to my old life I almost didn't lift a finger. At Ayda's insistence, I got off my butt and made a few phone calls. My lawyer back home was going to work on selling the house and my malpractice insurance was close to settling with the two patients who'd suffered for my problem with booze.

As far as my future was concerned, it's here with Ayda and the Saba-al-Bawdi.

Speaking of Ayda, she'd gone off to the lake-shore and set up an easel. Once I got the tent set up, I walked across our encampment, exchanging waves and smiles with everyone around me. The eight men who accompanied us on our raid of Sallah's place couldn't help themselves and told stories about how fast I moved or how I apparently calmed cages full of anxious dogs into silence... and, of course, they spoke of the People of the Sand.

Fortunately, none of them treated me like a celebrity or anything too embarrassing, more like I'd become one of the tribal elders or some kind of wise shaman.

Now, I walked up beside Ayda, and stopped short with two raised eyebrows at the image on her canvas: the vine-covered cliff plunging down into the lake. The same lake I'd leapt into in my not-quite-dream. She'd managed to capture it with almost photographic realism, so much so that I almost felt myself falling into the painting.

"That's…" I blinked. "How?"

She leaned into me, kissed me on the lips, and smiled. "When you described it to me, I saw it as though I stood there with you."

"Are you saying I planted it in your head or do you just have a vivid artist's imagination?"

"Does the how of it matter? Or, only that it is?" She kissed me on the cheek and resumed painting, adding a golden scorpion perched at the cliff's edge.

"You could do well as an artist in the 'civilized' world," I said, my tone jesting.

"You could do well in the civilized world as a dentist, as well. Yet here you are."

"Here I am." I brushed a hand over her hair.

War Baby ran over and nibbled on the hem of my robe, tugging and snarling, playing his little heart out. The younger children of the tribe all ran over, chasing him, and he flung himself into their open arms once again. All around us, the eyes of the Saba-al-Bawdi smiled at us. I'm sure all those old enough to think such thoughts assumed we would wed before the year was out.

And I can't say I'd mind that. Not at all.

Though I had given up the mantle of leadership, these people had become my family.

I had come halfway around the world to bring a

dog to his home.
    And found mine.

The End

Author's Note:

The country of East Sahara does not exist. Nor does the "desert shepherd" dog breed. Most of this book is a figment of my overactive imagination... a book that has been in the works since 2003. As of this publication date, that's 16 years. A version of this story appears in my short story collection, *Dark Rain*, under the title "War Daddy." Thank you for reading. I hope you enjoyed my tale of love, hope and redemption. As the big bundle of white fur and slobber himself would say, "Woof woof."

Translation: "Much love."

I happen to agree. Much love from War Daddy and me.

—J.R.

About J.R. Rain:

J.R. Rain is the international bestselling author of over seventy novels, including his popular Samantha Moon and Jim Knighthorse series. His books are published in five languages in twelve countries, and he has sold more than 3 million copies worldwide.

Please find him at: www.jrrain.com.